THE REGULATORS

by

Elliot Conway

Dales Large Print Books
Long Preston, North Yorkshire,
BD23 4ND, England.

British Library Cataloguing in Publication Data.

Conway, Elliot
    The regulators.

    A catalogue record of this book is
    available from the British Library

    ISBN   1-84262-062-2 pbk

First published in Great Britain 1999 by Robert Hale Limited

Copyright © Elliot Conway 1999

Cover illustration © Ballestar by arrangement with
Norma Editorial S.A.

The right of Elliot Conway to be identified as the author of this
work has been asserted by him in accordance with the
Copyright, Designs and Patents Act, 1988

Published in Large Print 2001 by arrangement with
Robert Hale Limited

Dales Large Print is an imprint of Library Magna Books Ltd.

Printed and bound in Great Britain by
T.J. (International) Ltd., Cornwall, PL28 8RW

One

There were two men at the camp on the small creek that snaked its way beneath a red-faced craggy butte. The big, beefy man lay with his back resting against a rock, hat tipped over his face shielding his eyes from the sun. The smaller, much leaner man, sat closer to the fire, rubbing at the working parts of a fifteen-load Winchester with an oily rag.

'Riders comin' in, Murdoch,' the small man said conversationally, without pausing in the cleaning of his rifle.

'I see 'em, Skeeter,' the big man growled 'I ain't asleep. I was just thinkin' we're m'be gettin' too old for this regulatin' business.'

Skeeter laughed. 'What the hell do you want us to do, have us tend woollies?'

'Could do worse, *amigo*, could do worse,'

replied Murdoch. 'At least sheep don't shoot back. And as I said, we ain't gettin' any younger.' Straightening up his hat he heaved himself on to his feet with the ease of a man half his bulk and looked at the rapidly closing cloud of trail dust, then he spoke again. 'There's two of them, Skeeter. One of them could be the man who's payin' our wages.' He cold-smiled at his partner. 'Or they could be Montana bad-asses comin' to rob two trail-weary travellers.' His hand dropped to the butt of the .44 Walker Colt resting in an open-flapped cavalry holster hanging on a belt strapped to its last hole across his big belly.

Skeeter also stood up, keeping some distance from Murdoch, his smile matching his partner's in its iciness. 'Then they'll find we ain't *pacifico* sheepmen, Murdoch,' he said, levering a shell into the chamber of the Winchester.

Jeb Ritchie and his straw boss, Rod Bremen, drew up their horses just short of the camp. Ritchie, a thick-set, hard-faced man, close-eyed the men he had laid out good money for. The two regulators, who, according to the Cattlemen's Protective Association, were the best manhunters on their books.

Bremen was thinking his boss had wasted his cash. The small, weasel-faced regulator, wearing a store suit that looked as though it had been slept in since the day it had been bought, didn't have the cut of a top ranking manhunter. His big-gutted partner favoured Indian-style fringed and beaded buckskins. Bremen reckoned that the animal the hide had come from must have been skinned when Texas still belonged to the Mexicans. In no way could he picture him ass-kicking his horse, exchanging lead with a bunch of rustlers. In his considered opinion, the big barrel of lard would be hard pressed to climb into his saddle. Bremen registered his feelings by spitting between his horse's ears.

Ritchie was seeing a different, more optimistic picture of the pair. He had been running a spread for more than thirty years.

Ten years ago he had driven a herd of longhorns all the way up from Texas to here in north Montana. He had hired, fired scores of ranch-hands of all temperaments and colours. His golden rule when hiring men, so as to get a feeling of the hand's suitability to work for him, was to cheek on his horse and gear. If they showed the appearance of being looked after, the man was hired. A man who neglected his horse, gear and guns, essentials in keeping him alive on the plains, wouldn't raise any sweat worrying about how the cows in his charge were faring.

The coats of the three horses belonging to the men facing him shone with regular grain feeding and grooming. And their saddle gear, though old, glistened with an equally cared for look. Ritchie also noted, with grim satisfaction, the rifle the little man was holding just happened to be aimed at him and Bremen. It, like the horses' coats, shone with dedicated attention. The unshaven pair weren't exactly dressed to pay a call on some church ladies' sewing circle, but he hadn't hired them to make social calls. The big regulator gave a broad-faced smile that didn't soften his hard-eyed gaze one little bit.

'I take it you're Mr Ritchie,' Murdoch said. 'I'm Murdoch and the small gent there is Mr Skeeter.'

'I'm the fella who's hiring you,' Ritchie said, curtly. 'And this is my straw boss, Rod Bremen.' The rancher saw Mr Skeeter give him a slight nod and lower his rifle.

'I hope we haven't put you out none, Mr Ritchie, by makin' you ride all the way out here,' Murdoch said. 'It don't do to advertise our presence in the territory. We don't aim to give those rustlers any more edge than the sons-of-bitches have now.'

'Me and Mr Murdoch reckon to retire one day and tend woollies,' Skeeter said. 'Ain't that so, pard?'

An angry, perplexed-looking Ritchie glared at Bremen. Was the short-assed bastard ribbing him, he thought? Had he hired a couple of clowns? He switched his gaze back on to Skeeter but the shut-faced *hombre* was showing no signs of humour.

'It ain't exactly like Skeeter says, Mr Ritchie,' Murdoch said, on seeing the rancher's jaundiced-eyed look he was giving Skeeter. 'What he meant was we ain't goin' to get any retirement time in if the two of us show our hand and get jumped on by a whole passel of cattle-lifters. They can't be strung up twice for killin' us. And that situation won't stop your cows from bein' stolen.'

'Yeah, well, I can see your reason for keeping things just between us,' Ritchie said, calming down somewhat. 'You just point me in the direction of where the sonsuvbitches are holed-up and me and my boys will do the rest. If you need to get in touch with me, or I have any information for you, Mrs Meg Johnson, she runs the only rooming-house in Red Butte, will be our contact. Me and the widow-woman have a sort of arrangement going between us. She won't gab about your presence in the territory, Mr Murdoch.'

Meg Johnson, Murdoch thought. Him and Skeeter were once acquainted with a Meg Johnson, Big Meg, who ran a cathouse just north of the Kansas line. She and her girls served the horn-dog Texan drovers bringing up the herds along the Chisholm Trail to the railheads in Kansas. An arrangement with Big Meg those days cost four dollars. If the Widow Johnson was the Meg he knew he got to wondering how much she was charging Ritchie for his arrangement with her. Though it seemed she had changed her line of business now. In any case it was no business of his or Skeeter's, Big Meg was entitled to run her life the way she wanted.

'That's OK by me, Mr Ritchie,' he said. 'She could give us a run down on any strangers in Red Butte. We could show her some wanted flyers of rustlers who are still in business. She might m'be recognize some of them. Though in my opinion it will be a bunch of local boys who're takin' your stock.'

11

'Well, we know there's seven or eight of the sonsuvbitches.' Ritchie said. 'And they never lift more than thirty, forty head of stock, driving them north.'

'It's as Mr Ritchie states,' Bremen spoke for the first time. 'Me and the crew picked up their tracks. A big bunch of them, enablin' them to move the cows along fast. Then we lost their trail in the thick-timbered border country. We reckon the rustlers cross the Canadian line. Bed down the stock in some outa-the-way draw till they do the settlin' up with whoever's buyin' the cattle off them at Fort Whoop-up.'

Murdoch shot a quizzical glance at Skeeter. 'We ain't heard of a Fort Whoop-up before, have we, Mr Skeeter? Though not havin' operated this far north that ain't surprisin'.'

'It ain't a regular army post, or a proper trading station either,' the rancher replied. 'It's a robbers' roost with a fancy name up there in the wild lands beyond the Canadian border. I guess once it must have been the mountain men's rendezvous before the beaver were all trapped out of existence. Now it's a meeting place for gun-runners, whiskey peddlers, trading with the Indians on both sides of the border.' The rancher's voice rose in anger. 'And the bastards who are liftin' my stock!'

'Can't the ranchers in the territory raise up a posse and ride to those woods up north and burn down this so-called fort?' asked Skeeter.

'We don't exactly know where the blasted place is!' Ritchie snarled back. 'All we know is that Fort Whoop-up is in Canada. Even the Canadian redcoat lawmen don't know where it is. Though to be fair to the mounties they're a bit thin on the ground up there and they've got one hellva big piece of real estate to cover. And you can bet your bottom dollar the Canadian authorities won't take kindly to a bunch of armed-up Yankees fire-ballin' in on their bailiwick, even if we're only intent on doing their job for them.'

'I see your point, Mr Ritchie,' Murdoch said. 'Could cause what the Washington stuff-shirts call a diplomatic incident.' He grinned at the rancher. 'I opine me and Mr Skeeter scoutin' up there amongst those Canadian trees won't set off urgent Western Union wires between Washington and Montreal.'

You sure won't, Bremen thought sarcastically. He could see the Canadian lawmen throwing the pair in the nearest jail as suspected horse-thieves.

'But first we'll ride to Red Butte,' continued Murdoch. 'We intend using the town as our base. Make our acquaintance with the widow-woman, Mrs Johnson. Use her, if she's willin', as you suggest, Mr Ritchie, for us to keep in touch with you.' He favoured the rancher with another cold smile. 'You'll m'be not see us movin' around, but we'll be earnin' our pay. As you know already, cattle-lifters are sneaky sonsuvbitches to track down.'

After one last look at the two regulators

Ritchie gave them a curt nod and jerked his horse's head round. 'OK, Bremen,' he said. 'Let's go and leave these gents to go about their business, their bill is running up.'

'That fella, I reckon, Murdoch,' Skeeter said, when Ritchie and his straw boss had ridden out of earshot. 'Must run five, six thousand head of beef. Yet he's willin' to pay good money to catch men who are stealin' no more cows than he would expect to lose in the winter-time, or killed by wolves and suchlike varmints.'

'M'be so, m'be so, Skeeter,' Murdoch replied. 'But Ritchie is a proud man, more than likely sweated his balls off buildin' up his spread and naturally he don't like some asshole rustlers robbin' him. I remember Judge Roy Bean, way down there in Langtry, Texas, relating to me that he would hang a thief if he had only stolen one red cent with as much fervour of the right-eousness of his action as if the *hombre* had stolen a whole bankful of money. It's all a matter of principle.' He gave Skeeter an all-toothed smile. 'We've got principles, pard-ner, to see the cattle-lifters hung or shot come hell or high water. Now, let's break camp and press on to Red Butte to see if the Big Meg we once lusted after is the Meg Johnson who is sweet-smilin' Mr Ritchie.'

Two

Mitch Surtees, paunch-bellied, heavy jowelled-faced with fine living, was sitting at his private table in the Long Branch saloon partaking generously of a bottle of single malt Scotch. He reckoned it was celebration time. By now, way up in the Canadian backwoods, the problem he had been chewing over earlier on in the week should have been resolved.

Then he had been giving some serious thought to how he could make his other business enterprise more profitable, a query he could not put to any accountant to reason out for him – not when the business was trading in stolen cattle and horses. He had soon worked out his own solution of how to raise his profit margins by cutting down some of the overheads of the business. Like paying off Josh Purvis, his Canadian middle-man in the deal. Purvis wouldn't take kindly to being paid off, especially if he found out that the paying off he had in mind for his Canadian partner was several, fatal, loads of Colt shells in his hide.

He had had a good thing going with Purvis, a Canadian horse-stealer, such as exchanging cattle stolen from Montana ranchers for horses taken illegally from Canadian owners by Purvis and his gang. Surtees didn't actually steal the cows himself, that skilful operation was done by his hired hands, Tod Clanton and his gang of owlhoots, though his ranch, the Slash Y, was used as a holding place for the Canadian horses until a suitable buyer was found for them, naturally, with well-forged papers proving Slash Y ownership.

Cattle-lifting was a high-risk trade. If things went wrong he wouldn't just lose the lucrative dollars it brought in for him, he would lose his life. Being the owner of one of the biggest ranches in the state, big man in the political scene in the territory, wouldn't save him. If he was linked with a gang of rustlers he would only live as long as it took to sling a rope over a handy tree. So it made good business sense to him to see that the returns from the one-way-trip-to-Boot-Hill trade were as high as they could get. And Purvis, a fifty-fifty-split-partner was a heavy financial drain on the business that had to be curtailed, quickly.

Tod Clanton, a mean-eyed Missourian, a natural-born killer, and his straw boss, would, Surtees opined, see to it that Purvis was paid off, permanently. Then Brown Bear, Purvis's right-hand man, would take over the gang, at a much lower cut, he hoped.

It was a pity that things had to come to

this, Surtees thought. Purvis knew his business, he had kept a steady flow of stolen horses coming across the border, but there could be no sentimentality in a hard-nosed trade like rustling. Surtees drew out his big-faced, solid gold watch and checked the time. The Missourian had strong desires for Sue, a big-breasted blonde in the cathouse next door. He could wait till Clanton had cooled his blood more than somewhat. Then Clanton should be in a less ornery mood. Offering Clanton part of the cash he would save cutting out a fifty-fifty partner could, Surtees opined, win the Missourian over to the way he thought the business should be run in the future.

Tod Clanton, squatting on his heels in the brush at the side of the trail, looked at Bub Thorn, lying prone a few yards to his left. 'Remember, Bub,' he said, 'we've only got to down Purvis, but to make it look right we'll wing a couple of his boys.' Clanton grinned. 'We still need the gang to keep the horses comin' in.'

'Make sure that Purvis's boys don't know it's you who shot their boss,' Surtees had said, when he had told him about the new financial arrangements for the cattle-and-horse-lifting enterprise he was running.

No, he had thought, sneeringly, the fat son-of-a-bitch didn't want the 'breed to come across the line and lift his hair for his part in gunning down his boss. Though, to be fair, he wasn't keen to start a bloody vendetta with a bunch of wild back-woodsmen led by a part Sioux.

'Leave it to me and the boys,' he had told Surtees. 'We'll fix it so only Purvis will know for sure who's throwin' lead at him, just before I blow him outa his saddle.'

Now that time was about here. 'Don't forget to show yourself, Slats!' he called out.

Slats stepped clear of the brush opposite Clanton, showing him the red tunic and pointed, broad-brimmed hat he was wearing. Bub wolf-howled. 'You're a mite hairy about the face, Slats, for a Canadian mountie. But I reckon when we start cutting loose at them they'll be too busy gettin' the hell outa it to take a closer look at your ugly mug.'

'OK, boys,' Clanton said. 'Get back under cover and stay quiet. Purvis and his crew ain't a bunch of Eastern dudes; this is their own backyard we're in.' He levered a shell into the breech of the Winchester before crawling back into the brush.

Purvis was well pleased with the ease with which he and his boys had stolen the latest string of horses and the fact that no pursuers were ass-kicking it along their back trail. The dangerous part of the raid would soon be over, the handing over of the horses to the Yankees. After a few drinks and a session with the whores at Fort Whoop-up, they would set off on their return trip with the cattle, driving them bold-assed along the trail. Purvis smiled. After all he was a bona-fide cattle dealer; with papers to prove it. Good enough to fool any redcoat who hailed them. And after all, he thought, the mounties would be trying to hunt down a bunch of horse-thieves.

Clanton's truly aimed Winchester shell blew Purvis's thoughts, and most of his head, into oblivion in a single instant flash of blinding pain. Two more of the gang slumped low in their saddles, groaning with pain, clutching at shattered and bloody shoulders as Bub and Slats opened fire. The sudden burst of gunfire spooked the horses and they broke from the trail and stampeded headlong through the brush and the timber. The gang, just as panicky, flat on their mounts, pistols undrawn, followed in the wake of the horses.

Clanton got to his feet and looked across at Purvis's body lying in a tangle-limbed bundle on the trail. Purvis's horse was standing nearby. He walked across to it and searched through the saddle-bags then turned and faced Bub and Slats weighing a well-filled draw-string bag in his right hand. He grinned. 'We can hold a decent wake for the sonuvabitch back at the fort, boys. Now get him planted.'

'Planted!' said Bub. 'What the hell for? He ain't no buddy of mine!'

Clanton shot him a fish-eyed look. 'Because havin' gone to all the trouble of deckin' out Slats in a redcoat's tunic we have to keep up the pretence that it was the mounties who bushwhacked them. So ask yourself, would the mounties leave a body lyin' above ground, eh?' He gave Bub a toothy merciless smile. 'But you needn't say any prayers over the sonuvabitch.'

Clanton, Bub and Slats sat at a table in the big, weather-bleached, splay-planked shack that passed for a bar for the owlhoot fraternity who used Fort Whoop-up as a hideout when the law got too close to them on their own territories. The other members of the gang were guarding the stolen cattle they had driven to the fort from Montana.

Shooting Purvis hadn't caused Clanton any heartache, negotiating Surtees's deal with Brown Bear might not be so easy to pull off. The 'breed, part Sioux, what with seeing his boss gunned down, and thinking he could have gone the same way, and losing the horses and all, wouldn't be in a joyful, co-operative mood. More like a killing mood, Clanton thought.

The tricky bit of the deal he had to get across to Brown Bear, as sweet as he could, was for him to, unknowingly, accept a smaller cut of the pot than Purvis had been claiming, but, and he was banking on it, far more than Purvis had been paying him. If Purvis had been a generous payer then Surtees would have to up the ante – if Brown Bear let him stay alive to ride to Montana to see Surtees after trying to con him out of what should rightly be his.

Clanton heard the sounds of horses outside and a few seconds later the door burst open with a loud rasping of rusted hinges and Jules Brown Bear stormed into the shack, face twisted in mad-eyed rage. Clanton jerked upright in his chair, hand dropping on to the butt of his pistol, expecting the big, eagle-faced man to yank out the wicked-looking knife sheathed on his left hip and start cutting at him and the boys to work off some of his anger. The first flash of steel and he would plug the big son-of-a-bitch dead for sure and to hell with Surtees and his new business arrangements.

Following on behind the 'breed were the rest of the Canadians. Two, ashen-faced with pain, jacket sleeves dark with patches of blood were helped to chairs by the remaining three members of the gang. Brown Bear gave the three Yankees a glowering-eyed glare before grabbing a bottle of whiskey from the bar counter. Drawing out the cork with his teeth he took a long effortless swallow that almost emptied the bottle.

Clanton got to his feet. Facing a bad-assed part-Indian was bad enough; a liquored-up one was dicing with death. 'Hit trouble, Brown Bear?' he asked, face a false mask of concern.

Brown Bear swung round and eye-balled Clanton again. 'A redcoat patrol jumped us,' he snarled. 'The sonsuvbitches blew Josh's head clear off. Wounded Lafe and Jacques there.' His face became all Sioux, glaring and savage. Clanton's hand twitched nervously above his pistol. 'And the horses we were bringin' in are scattered all through the goddamned woods!' Brown Bear spat the words out.

'The mounties ain't trailed you here, have they?' Clanton said. He drew his pistol and made for the door, giving a good impression, he thought, of a man expecting shooting trouble.

Brown Bear gave Clanton a fish-eyed look. 'I ain't some city greenhorn!' he snapped. 'I checked we weren't bein' tailed.'

Clanton slipped his gun back into its holster. 'Well that's a relief,' he said. 'Your mounties work differently to our marshals. Those redcoats fight as though they're blasted soldier-boys.' He close-eyed Brown Bear. 'I'm hopin' that your brush with them, and Josh bein' killed, won't stop you from keepin' our deal goin'. The boss will naturally see to it that you get the same cut as Josh had.' The false look of concern came back on to his face. 'If you ain't willin' to take over the gang then you've left me one helluva problem. Like leavin' me with a bunch of cows I can't drive back to Montana without riskin' a hangin' for me and my boys.'

Brown Bear did some fast thinking, hard-eying Clanton as he did so. There were no banks or stages to rob this close to the border, so the only way he could earn some much wanted cash was to steal horses, to carry on dealing with Clanton. But if his gut-feelings were proved right, and Clanton was trying to put one over him, thinking that being a 'breed he wasn't as sharp in business deals as Purvis had been, he would lift the forked-tongued son-of-a-bitch's hair and go and find a train to rob.

'How much was Josh's cut?' he asked.

Clanton was all smiles inside. Surtees's

deal was going to go through a damn sight smoother than he had thought. It looked as no blood was going to be shed on either side. The grabbing bastard, Purvis, hadn't told the 'breed he was on a fifty-fifty split with Surtees. He had been getting away with paying his boys just enough to keep them happy. He felt he could lower Surtees's offer somewhat.

'Purvis had twenty per cent of what we made on the whole deal,' he lied, as open-faced as an altar boy. Surtees was willing to part with twenty-five per cent of the takings, the difference, Clanton thought, was better in his pocket. He leered knowingly at Brown Bear. 'What you pay your boys is your concern,' he said, and noticed the greedy glint at the back of the 'breed's eyes. He was working out how much of the cut he could keep back for himself without his boys becoming suspicious and gunning him down for being a no-good cheat.

Grinning wryly, Clanton laid on the mock sympathy. 'I know you ain't got any horses to trade,' he said. 'But it weren't your doin' you lost them, so to show good faith in our new partnership you can have the cows we've brought in. Split what you get for them with your crew so they'll stick by you; I've got genuine forged bills of sale for them. Normally me and Purvis used to show each what we got for sellin' the stock so neither of us could get bad thoughts that we were tryin' to short change each other. We'll arrange to do that once we get tradin' regularly.'

Brown Bear was still having the feeling that the snake-eyed Clanton was going to get the better of the deal, but then again, he thought, he was going to make more than Purvis had been paying him. If he wanted to stay in the rustling business he had to take it. 'We've got ourselves a deal goin' between us,' he said.

'Good,' said Clanton, opining the 'breed had swallowed a lot of his pride in accepting the deal. He could swallow what the hell he liked, he thought, as long as he kept the horses coming in.

It was a much smiling Clanton who rode out of Fort Whoop-up with his boys, with the high hopes of being much richer.

Three

On crossing the creek, Skeeter and Murdoch hit a well-travelled trail that led in the direction of the township named after the towering red-faced rock now at their backs, a way that rose steadily to a long, rocky ridge.

Before reaching the rimline they heard the sudden rattle of gunfire beyond it. Exchanging, 'What the hell glances' they kneed their horses into a brisk canter, pulling them up just short of where the trail dipped down the reverse slope. With the experience of men who had partnered each other through many violent times, neither of them had to ask each other who did what. Skeeter drew out his rifle and swung down from his mount and ran to the ridge dropping down flat to the ground to belly crawl the last few paces to the edge. The big man, whose eyes weren't as keen as his partner's stayed up on his horse, holding on to Skeeter's and the pack-horse's reins.

Below Skeeter the trail dipped as easily on to a vast stretch of flats and he picked out the heat-blurred smudges of a scattering of buildings on the distant horizon which he took to be Red Butte. Much nearer, he saw the wagon, minus one of its rear wheels, slewed across the trail. Three guns were firing at the broken-down wagon, two on one side of the trail, covering the third man sneaking closer to the wagon through the rocks and brush on the opposite side of the trail.

The firing from beneath the wagon was from two guns, a pistol and, spasmodically, a double-barrelled riot gun. Skeeter took a closer look at who was being attacked. His face grimmed over and he sidled back from the edge, got to his feet and hurried down to Murdoch. 'Get your big ass off your horse, Murdoch,' he said. 'There's a coupla folk over the ridge who need our help.' Then told him about the attack on the wagon.

Murdoch stayed put in the saddle. 'Skeeter,' he said, 'we ain't Samaritans. Stoppin' gunfights on the trail ain't our business. That's the job for badge-totin' marshals. We've hard-assed it all this way to rope in a bunch of cattle-lifters. If we do poke our nose in the affair whose side do we come in on, eh? The two *hombres* under the wagon could be *desperadoes* resistin' arrest.'

'Could be, Murdoch,' conceded Skeeter. 'Though one of them would be a female *desperado.*'

'A female!' repeated Murdoch, eyebrows raised in surprise.

Skeeter grinned. 'Yeah, unless bad-asses in Montana are takin' to wearing skirts and look like Big Meg.'

'Big Meg!' said Murdoch, dismounting as

though his ass was on fire. He reached up and yanked his Winchester out of its boot. 'What the hell are we wastin' time jawin' here!' he growled. 'Let's go and shoot us some *desperadoes!*'

Big Meg, flat on her stomach beneath the wagon, gasped sharply with pain as splinters of wood ripped off the wagon bottom drew blood on her face. Cursing she reloaded the shotgun with the last two shells she had then thumbed back the twin hammers. More angry than scared she waited for clear sighting of the men who had dry-gulched them so she could pepper their dirty hides with lead.

She thin-smiled across at Luke Sanders, the old man who helped at her rooming-house, low down behind the front wheel of the wagon. Though wounded in the shoulder he was keeping up a steady rate of fire from a big cap and ball pistol that must have been as old as he was. Its loud discharge and the heavy double boom of the shotgun was showering her with dust from the underside of the wagon and making her head ring. Big Meg chewed savagely at her lower lip. Damn it, she thought, angrily, she wouldn't shoot the first of the bastards she saw, she would run out and beat the hell out of him with the gun for all the discomfort they were putting her through. Big Meg did some more dirty-mouthing.

Luke hadn't had any close dealings with women, apart from the occasional trip he made to the cathouse. He certainly had never been partnered by a female in a 'between a rock and a hard place' situation before. Big Meg must know what her fate would be once their ammunition ran out and the border scum rushed in for the kill. Yet there she was cursing like a drunken mule-skinner and as savage-faced as any Sioux buck he had exchanged lead with along the Powder when scouting for General 'Bear Coat' Nelson Miles. No sir, he thought. Miss Meg was sure no handicap for a man when the chips were down.

'You'd better keep those two loads for the

sonuvabitch who's sneakin' in behind us, Miss Meg,' he said. 'His two pards in front are only keepin' us occupied.'

'Never fear, Luke,' Big Meg replied. 'I'm lookin' forward to pullin' off two shells at him.' Then she added, hopefully, 'M'be someone will come ridin' along the trail and scare them off.'

'M'be,' said Luke, trying to sound convincing to keep his boss's spirits up. The three of them would come in with a rush, firing and yelling soon. It would take a miracle to prevent that from happening and Luke, not being a praying man, didn't believe in suchlike events.

Murdoch drew a bead on the only bushwhacker he could see, and that was just his legs. Wounding him, would, he hoped, cause his buddies to have second thoughts about raiding the wagon and hightail it to try their luck someplace else. Otherwise it could be a long drawn-out gunfight. By now, he calculated, Skeeter, after ass-sliding down a nearby gully, would be all set to take on the single raider coming on to the wagon from the left. He bared his teeth in a merciless grin. It was time he started the war before Big Meg got hurt. Gently he squeezed the Winchester trigger.

He heard, clearly, the high-pitched scream of pain from his target and saw one of his legs kick out wildly. The raider wouldn't be able to move his other leg, maybe not ever, if the shattered kneecap didn't mend right.

Luke's face split in a grin. 'That's the sound of a long gun, Miss Meg,' he said. 'And one of those bastards out there is hurt real bad.' Big Meg shuddered, then thankfully the blood-curdling cries suddenly stopped.

'You pilgrims down there!' Murdoch yelled. 'Bein' that I'm in a charitable mood I'll allow you to get your wounded buddy on to his horse. If you're stubborn-minded and want to stay and make a fight of it then when I cut loose with this Winchester again I'll be aimin' to kill!'

Murdoch couldn't see the other raider at

first then a man came running out of the brush. He looked up, fearfully, at the ridge, raising his arms wide and high to show that he was unarmed before half-carrying, half-dragging his now unconscious partner away. A few minutes later, Murdoch saw two horses with riders up raising the dust northwards. He gave a grunt of satisfaction and turned his attention to where Skeeter and the last raider were.

The third raider on hearing the hair-raising scream, ate dirt, his face twisting with fear. Easy picking of two horses and the free use of a fine-looking female didn't look so good now. He began to wriggle backwards the way he had come to make for his horse and get to hell out of it, fast, but making sure he didn't show himself to the sharp-shooting bastard on the ridge who had done for Pete.

'You ain't about to pull-out, friend, just because the goin's got rough for you and your buddies,' Skeeter said, conversationally.

The raider screwed round on his chest and found himself eyeballing a pistol held on him by a small, foxy-faced man squatting on his heels a few paces away from him, and grinning as though it were a friendly get-together.

Skeeter caught a glimpse of the look in the raider's eyes, the flashing wildness of a desperate, last chance gamble. He fired as the raider swung his gun on to him. The smashing impact of the .44 ball at point-blank range in the chest lifted the man inches from the ground to slam him back to the dirt, arms outstretched, a dead man.

'Are you OK, Skeeter?' he heard Murdoch call out. 'The other two have hightailed it!'

Skeeter got to his feet in clear sighting of Murdoch. 'Kind of you to worry about me, pardner. I'm OK but I've got a dead man here. He chose the hard way to go. Bring the horses down and I'll meet you at the wagon! Big Meg, the shootin's over, me and Murdoch are comin' in!'

'Well I'll be durned!' Meg gasped 'Skeeter

and Murdoch!' It must be over two years since she had last seen Skeeter and his big gorilla of a partner. She thought the pair would have ended up on some Boot Hill by now with the trade they followed. Some poor rustlers hereabouts would be soon attending a necktie party, as the main guests. She grinned at Luke. 'They're friends of mine from way back,' and began scrambling out from beneath the wagon.

By the time Skeeter reached the wagon, burdened with an extra gunbelt draped over his shoulder, Meg had brushed as much dust from her clothes with her hands as she could and fluffed up her hair. Though she was somewhat heavier round her ass and up front nowadays, she didn't want Skeeter and Murdoch to think that because she had quit being a whore she had let herself go to seed.

Big Meg smiled. Skeeter still dressed like a man who had gone to the dogs a long time ago. Many a cattle-lifter had been fooled by Skeeter's and Murdoch's saddle-tramp looks, ending up under the hanging tree.

Skeeter smiled and touched the brim of his hat at her, giving Luke an acknowledging tilt of his head.

'Ain't it a small world, Meg?' he said.

'It sure is, Mr Skeeter,' Meg replied, all smiles.

'Amen to that, Mr Skeeter,' Luke said. 'In fact if it had been a mite bigger me and Miss Meg could've been dead.'

'This is Luke Sanders, Skeeter,' Meg said. 'He helps out at a rooming-house I own in Red Butte, a town three, four miles ahead of us. The bits and pieces you see on the wagon I've bought from a homesteader who's had enough tryin' to make corn grow in dirt. Then as you can see, the wagon axle snapped and Luke was loosening one of the horses to ride on to town and bring out the blacksmith when those three sons-of-bitches jumped us. Now what about you and Murdoch, what are you doing this far north? Still scratchin' around for a living?'

'Yeah, me and the big fella have taken up pannin' for gold,' Skeeter replied, pleased to discover that Big Meg wasn't a loose-mouth and hadn't blown his and Murdoch's cover. He grinned at Big Meg. 'I hope we strike a motherlode soon; Murdoch's feelin' his age and has a hankerin' to raise some woollies before he's laid out for plantin'.'

Murdoch came down on to the flat with the horses and drew up at the wagon. Luke gave him a quick but noting look. Like his small partner he had the appearance of a man who hadn't slept in a real bed under a roof for quite a spell. In keeping, he thought, with men who claimed they panned for paydirt along the banks of streams in the high country A few minutes ago, Miss Meg's face reminded him of a war-painted-up Sioux buck's face. He was getting the same chilly feelings about Mr Murdoch and Mr Skeeter. Their glances were as hard-eyed and all-seeing as any Indian's. Too much so for two drifters. But it was no business of his what the pair really did for a living. They had saved his and Miss Meg's life, and that was all that mattered.

Murdoch favoured Big Meg with a big moon-faced smile as he dismounted. 'You're still as purty as when me and Skeeter first set eyes on you.'

Skeeter gave Murdoch a significant look. 'I was tellin' Meg that we're goin' to try our luck at pannin' for gold along the Canadian border so we can sit on the front porch countin' our sheep.'

'Ain't that the truth, Skeeter,' Murdoch said. 'Neither of us is as young as we were, Meg.'

'There ain't no disagreement there, Murdoch,' Meg said, smiling. 'But it was handsomely done the way you got those road agents off me and Luke's back. And I am beholden to you for putting yourselves out to come and help us.'

'Think nothin' of it, Meg,' Murdoch replied. 'That's what friends are for, ain't it?' He turned and faced Luke. 'I see they've winged you, Mr Sanders.'

'It ain't much,' Luke said. 'And it won't stop me doin' what I was intendin' to do before we got bushwhacked, ride into town and haul out the blacksmith.'

'You do that, Luke,' Meg said. 'And get your arm seen to before you ride back. Me and the boys here will get the wagon unloaded ready for the smith to work on the axle.'

'OK, Miss Meg,' Luke said. He nodded to Skeeter and Murdoch. 'Thanks again, gents. Like the boss, I'm beholden to you. If there's anything I can do for you don't hesitate to look me up. I ain't hard to find, Miss Meg runs the only roomin'-house in Red Butte.'

'There is something you can do for us, Luke,' Skeeter said. 'Don't mention our part in this business. The law will want to talk to us and we'll be pointed out in town. The two we drove off could have blood kin and me and Murdoch could be walkin' into a lion's den when we head into the back country.'

Luke grinned at Skeeter. 'If you bury that fella you plugged, Mr Skeeter, and I say that

I accidentally shot myself cleanin' my gun then we ain't had anything more serious happen here than that busted axle.'

'That sounds fine to me, Mr Sanders,' Skeeter said, 'if you can stand the ribbin' you'll get in the saloons for bein' so foolish as to shoot yourself.'

'You're here to stop the rustling that's going on in the territory,' Meg said, when Luke had ridden off. 'Mr Ritchie, he owns the Double Circle ranch has asked the Cattlemen's Protective Association to send in regulators to clear up the trouble.'

'We've already met Mr Ritchie, Meg,' Skeeter said. 'And he told us he had some sort of an arrangement with you. Close enough it seems for him to trust you to be our contact with him if we need any of his boys to help us out. Or he has any fresh information about the men we're tryin' to track down.'

'It ain't really any business of ours, Meg,' Murdoch said. 'But me bein' a nosy sonuvabitch I was wonderin' if Mr Ritchie knows you were once a whorehouse madam, him bein' a Texan and must have brung cattle up the trail to Kansas.'

Big Meg laughed. 'Good Lord, no! I've led him to believe I'm a widow-woman. Told him I came here to escape the Texas Indians who killed my "man", and the Texas dust. I know he's a Texan, Murdoch, but me and my girls didn't serve every goddamned horndog Texan drover who came up the Chisholm Trail.' Meg sighed. 'Though sometimes it felt as though we did.'

Skeeter gave her a flint-eyed look. 'We ain't overjoyed usin' you as go-between, Meg,' he said. 'The business me and Murdoch are embarked on is between us, Ritchie and the cattle-lifters, killin'-men's business.'

Face just as serious, Meg said, 'I've faced stompin' men before, I'll take care.' Her expression lightened up. 'I reckon no cattle-lifter would raise a suspicious eyebrow if he noticed two strangers to Red Butte calling at the only rooming-house in town. You two saddletramps look as though a good, home-cooked meal wouldn't come amiss.' Meg wrinkled her nose. 'Or an hour's soaking in a hot tub.'

Skeeter grinned at Murdoch. 'We wouldn't say no to both of those suggestions, Meg. We've been wonderin' why the horses stay well up wind of us when we make camp.' His face hardened. 'We'd be interested to know what the situation is in Red Butte, cattle-wise, that is, Meg.'

'Well there's little I can tell you that's out of the ordinary, Skeeter,' Meg said. 'Red Butte's like any other cow town, be it in Texas or Kansas. There's eight, nine spreads scattered across the territory. Jeb Ritchie's ranch is the largest. The next is the Slash Y owned by Mitch Surtees.' Meg paused for a moment or two as she gave deeper thought to things she had previously taken as normal. 'Well there's the Slash Y crew,' she began, hesitantly. 'I don't know if it's significant or not.'

'You tell us what's on your mind, Meg,' Murdoch said. 'You've been around cow towns long enough to have an opinion worth listenin' to.'

'I know ranch-hands aren't *hombres* an old maid would invite into her parlour for tea and cookies, but Surtees's boys seem a mite more hard-nosed breed of men. It wouldn't surprise me if some of their likenesses were decorating wanted flyers.' Meg shrugged her shoulders. Half-smiling she said, 'That's it, boys. I don't know if it is of any help. All I know is it's a bad feeling I get when I see the Slash Y crew in Red Butte.'

'Me and Murdoch are enterin' this situation blindfolded, Meg,' Skeeter said. 'Any information is gratefully received. Time will tell whether it's significant or not. Now let's get that fella planted and the wagon unloaded, Murdoch. We don't want to be standin' here when Luke returns with the blacksmith.' He saw the look of alarm come into Meg's face. 'You needn't fret, Meg,' he said. 'We'll be up on the ridge back there lookin' out for you till this wagon of yours is rollin' along the trail to Red Butte.' He smiled at Meg. 'And we'll give this fella Surtees's crew a closer look. Now, Murdoch, take off your coat and let's raise some sweat.'

Four

'So everything went OK, Clanton?' Mitch Surtees said.

Clanton, sitting in the rancher's den in the Slash Y big house, grinned across the desk at Surtees. 'The 'breed bought it,' he said. 'Though he wasn't too happy about his cut he knows he can't make as much spendin' money any easier. He'll keep liftin' the horses for us. We lost the last string they were bringin' up to Fort Whoop-up. Me and the boys could've rounded-up some of them but I figured it was too risky. The part-Injun ain't no fool. I couldn't take the chance that the 'breed, or one of his boys recognizing Slats's ugly mug bein' very much like the mountie's face. The 'breed, puttin' two and two together could see me hangin' head first over a slow fire. So I thought it wise to bring the boys back so as not to jog the Canadians' memories.'

'It's worth losing a few horses to keep a profitable business going, Clanton,' Surtees said. He hard-eyed Clanton. 'But it don't do to get complacent. While you were away I had a drink with the Western Union field manager. He told me that Ritchie of the Double Circle has sent a wire to the Cattlemen's Protective Association in Denver asking them help to track down the men who are stealing his cattle. So already there could be association regulators snooping around in the territory. It would be healthier for us to keep an eye on Ritchie when he's in town, and who he speaks to.' Surtees's face hardened. 'If they're strangers to Red Butte you pass the time of day with them, and make it the last words they hear if you suspect them of being regulators. You get my drift, Clanton?'

'I'll have a coupla boys ride into town, Mr Surtees,' Clanton said, as determined as his boss that no regulator was going to put an end to the good deal he had struck with the 'breed, or put his head in a noose.

'Good,' said Surtees. 'Have them keep an eye on the rooming-house. Ritchie, I hear, has the hots for the big-breasted widow-woman who owns it. The sonuvabitch won't want to meet the men he's hiring in the open.'

Clanton pushed back his chair and got to his feet. 'There won't be so much as a stray dog comin' into Red Butte without bein' checked out,' he said, face as hard as his boss's. 'You have my word on it.'

Skeeter and Murdoch rode slowly along Main Street, Red Butte. Slouch-backed in the saddle, hats tilted over faces, they had the appearance of men at ease with the world. But eyes half-hidden by hat brims were taking in and cataloguing everything they saw. They dismounted outside the livery barn, Murdoch staying with the horses while Skeeter entered the barn to see if there was space for the animals. Murdoch began to check the load ropes on the packhorse, an excuse to beady-eye a man standing across the street, trying hard not to look in his direction.

'If you want any work doin,' mister,' a young boy told Skeeter, 'you'll have to wait till my pa, he's the blacksmith, comes back. He's out fixin' Mrs Johnson's wagon back along the trail a piece.'

Skeeter could have told the boy that his pa had fixed the wagon, good enough to make it to town, fifteen, twenty minutes behind them on the trail. As they had promised, he and Murdoch had stayed on the ridge till Luke had returned with the blacksmith, waiting till the smith had got the wagon back on the road again. Only then did they move out, circling well clear of the trail, making it to Red Butte before the slow-moving wagon.

'I don't want any jobs doin', boy,' Skeeter said. 'There's three horses outside that need feedin' and beddin' down for the night. Me and my pard are movin' out in the mornin'. Prospectin' for gold up in the border country. And I'd like a safe place where we could stow our gear. Otherwise we'll have to tote it along to the roomin'-house we passed on the way here.'

Skeeter came out of the barn and told Murdoch the horses would be attended to and their gear stored behind padlocked doors. 'So let's get them inside,' he said. 'And get along to the roomin'-house and that meal Big Meg promised to cook for us.' He took hold of his horse's reins to lead it into the barn.

Once through the barn doors, Murdoch growled, 'I'm gettin' a strong feelin', Skeeter, there's other than Big Meg in this dog-dirt burg expectin' regulators bein' on their way here. There's an *hombre* across the street, though he's tryin' hard not to show it, is givin' us a good eyeballin'. Of course, I m'be wrong; I might be sufferin' from that complaint I once read about in a book, persecution complex I think they called it. That's when an *hombre* gets to thinkin' that the whole world is agin him.'

Skeeter smiled thinly. 'Ain't that the way we always feel, Murdoch? How the hell have we stayed alive all this time in our line of business, eh? By treatin' everyone we meet on the trail as long lost blood kin? We'll take it for granted then that Mr Ritchie has been loose-mouthin' about his sendin' for regulators. Though that don't mean we're in any imminent danger, it'll pay us to walk softly.' Skeeter's smile broadened. 'Times like this, Murdoch I've got to admit, make tendin' sheep not so bad after all.'

Bub had orders from Clanton to treat every stranger riding into town as possible undercover Cattlemen's Association agents. The big fat man, garbed in tattered buckskins, and his small, weasel-faced partner hadn't the look of irregular lawmen. Bub had seen regulators and Pinkertons before. Most of them were bowler-hatted, clean-shirted, city-suited men, men who snooped around asking nosy questions. Any trackin' to be done, the sons-of-bitches hired trackers to read sign for them.

The sieves, pans, picks and spades dangling down both sides of the packhorse fitted in with the pair's ragged-assed appearance of high-country pay-dirt seekers. Still, to ease the uncomfortable tightness around his neck since he had heard of the probability of regulators showing up in Red Butte he would keep a sharp eye on them.

Bub watched them walking along the boardwalk with their saddle-bags slung over their shoulders, heading, he opined, for the rooming-house. Slats was watching the coming and goings at the widow-woman's rooming-house. He would follow the gold seekers and ask Slats his opinion on the pair. It looked as though they were staying at least one night in town. Maybe that would give him time to have someone sneak into their rooms and check out what was in their saddle-bags. They could hold papers relating to who they were.

The furniture on the wagon was being unloaded by Luke, the blacksmith and two other men when Skeeter and Murdoch stepped on to the porch of the rooming-house. Big Meg was nowhere in sight. Cooking that meal for them, they both hoped.

'There's another fella over there, Skeeter,' Murdoch said, out of the side of his mouth. 'Tryin' to look as though he's idlin' his time away. So whoever's hirin' him must know where Mr Ritchie spends some of his leisure time, and where he could meet, private-like, any regulator. Or so Ritchie thought.'

Skeeter's face Indianed over. 'And that puts an end to Big Meg actin' as our go-between. We ain't goin' to get her involved in our dirty business, Murdoch, that's for sure. I never cottoned on to the idea from the start. It's us who's paid to take all the risks. If we want to meet up with Ritchie we'll choose our own time and place, OK?'

'My thoughts entirely, pard,' replied Murdoch.

A smiling Big Meg greeted them inside. 'I'm sorry the meal isn't cooked yet,' she apologized. 'You can see we've just got here. The smith had to take it easy on the trail comin' in or the wheel would have come off again. But there's plenty of hot water ready in the boiler. The bathroom is the building out back, two tubs, so there's no need to come to blows who uses the water first. By the time you've both had a good soak the grub should be on the table. And if you want any clothes washing just leave 'em out, I'll see to them.' Then Big Meg noticed their stone-faced looks. 'Trouble?' she asked, her smile fading rapidly.

Skeeter shook his head. 'Not yet, Meg,' he said. 'More like an inconvenience. You just take a peek outa that window and see if you can put a name to that fella standin' on the opposite boardwalk.'

A curious-eyed Meg walked over to the window and standing at one side, lifted a corner of the drapes slightly and looked out. She turned and faced Skeeter and Murdoch before saying, 'There's two of them there now. I don't know their names but they're Slash Y men.' She hard-eyed Murdoch and Skeeter. 'Well, aren't you goin' to tell me what's goin' on then?' she snapped.

Skeeter ignored her pleas. 'Slash Y, boys,' he murmured, more to himself than to Murdoch or Big Meg. 'That's Surtees's tough-lookin' crew you told me and Murdoch about, Meg?'

'Damn it, Skeeter!' Meg exploded angrily. 'Aren't you listenin'? I asked you what was goin' on!'

'What's goin' on, Meg,' Skeeter replied soothingly, 'is that me and Murdoch reckon that somehow Surtees knows about your boyfriend sending for us. How he did find out don't matter. What matters to us is why Surtees's interested in us. So interested that he's posted two of his boys watchin' places where men who could be regulators ridin' into town would first show up, the livery barn, and the only roomin'-house in Red Butte.'

'Bein' suspicious *hombres*, Meg,' Murdoch said, 'me and Skeeter have to take it that those two hardcases across the street ain't part of a joyous welcomin' committee for any regulator comin' in.'

Meg gasped. 'You mean Surtees is the man at the back of the rustling going on in the territory!'

'He's made himself our number-one suspect, Meg,' Skeeter said. 'All we've got to do is prove our suspicions, strong enough to hold up in a court of law.'

'Or catch his boys actually stealin' cows,' Murdoch added. He wolf-smiled. 'Then we can kinda cut a few legal corners so to speak, Meg. By pluggin' them dead or hanging 'em high. One thing is for sure we won't be usin' you as our contact with Ritchie, or stay here more than one night.

Surtees's men are on the prowl and men facin' a hangin' ain't particular who they hurt to save their dirty hides. If they're suspicious of us they'll be suspicious of who we talk to. And you could get hurt real bad. Me and Skeeter are paid to take all the hassle we might raise in our snoopin' around.'

Meg could see the sense of what Murdoch had said. Glum-faced she said, 'And I was hoping to feed you boys up and talk about the old days.'

Skeeter grinned. 'Life gets downright hard sometimes, Meg, as you oughta know.' His smile became icy. 'As those sonsuvbitches cattle-lifters are soon goin' to find out.'

'But don't you let on to Ritchie our suspicions, Meg,' Murdoch said, warningly. 'By what we've seen of Ritchie he's a tetchy character. Could start a range war between him and Surtees and get some of his boys killed. It's as Skeeter says, we're the boys up front. Now that's enough yappin'; I swear I've never spoken as many words in the past six months. Let's go and have that bath, Skeeter, then we can partake of that chow I can smell cookin'. Then we'll pay a visit to a few of the saloons and act for the benefit of those assholes watchin' us, like real highcountry gold-seekers, by gettin' roarin' drunk. And m'be hire the services of a lewd woman.' He grinned at Meg. 'I take it there is such-like females in Red Butte? Or has the town got religion?'

'Two blocks down, Murdoch,' Big Meg said, smilingly. 'Though speaking professionally they ain't as good as my girls were, but good enough for two wild-assed, highcountry boys.'

Murdoch looked at Skeeter as his partner refilled his glass with a hand that shook, spilling some of the whiskey on the table, their second bottle since entering the Long Branch saloon. They had cleaned themselves up, eaten well and with the not required warning from Big Meg to take care, they headed for the nearest bar to show themselves to the interested parties that they were what they looked, down-at-the-heel gold-seekers.

Skeeter's face had the pinched-assed visage of a mean drunk man. He wore his gunbelt strapped on the outside of his coat; the pistol holstered on his left hip, butt outwards, was balanced by a big Green River knife held in a beaded sheath on his right side. He had the nervous twitching movements of a man, who if looked unkindly on, would yank out both his weapons and indulge in a shooting and stabbing spree any liquored-up Sioux would be proud of.

He frightened Murdoch and the big man knew Skeeter was only putting on an act. Small as he was, Skeeter could down the coal oil that passed for drinking man's liquor in the Long Branch by the barrelful and still remain sober. The show was for the two Slash Y men sitting several tables away. The pair had been joined by a third man, a character Murdoch easily catalogued. The original pair may fancy themselves as prodding men but their companion was the genuine article. As mean-looking as Skeeter, only for real. He might be working on a cattle spread but Murdoch opined killing was his real trade. He also reckoned it was time he played his part in the game.

'Now don't go and get yourself crazy drunk, Skeeter,' he said, loud enough for their trailers to hear, 'or I'll have to bend the barrel of my Colt over your dumb head. You know we're movin' out early tomorrow and I want to spend some time in the cathouse, not in the jailhouse. And that's where we'll end up in if you cause any trouble here.'

'I told you that those two bums ain't regulators, Tod,' Bub said. 'Why, the small guy has downed enough whiskey to send a whole tribe of Injuns on a hair-liftin' raid. And you heard the big ape say they're leavin' town tomorrow.' Bub laughed. 'The state the pair will be in before they make it back to the roomin'-house, they couldn't find gold in Fort Knox.'

'It looks that way,' Clanton said. He gave Bub and Slats a gimlet-eyed look. 'But we can't afford to take chances. Regulators are on their way here, or are already in Red Butte. Surtees said we had to check out every stranger in town real good, and that makes sense. If they go to the cathouse, you tail them, Bub. Check out that they're not usin' the visit as an excuse to meet up with Ritchie of the Double Circle. Accordin' to Surtees he's the sonuvabitch who's siccin the regulators on us.'

Bub would have liked to tell Clanton that they had watched the two panhandlers long enough to satisfy Surtees and the whole damn population of Red Butte that they weren't regulators. Tell him that him and Slats had some serious drinking and fooling-around-with-women business to do before their next raid. That is if he had the balls to go against Clanton's sayso. Clanton, he knew, wasn't a man who could be sweet-talked out of his way of thinking. When the Missourian ex-guerilla said jump you did that or quit the gang. If you were lucky you could get up on to your horse and ride away.

'OK, Tod, I'll do that,' he said. Then, turning to Slats, he added, 'When I see them bedded down in the cathouse I'll see you back here, then we can start drinkin' for real.'

'Do you think we've fooled them, Murdoch?' Skeeter hissed.

'Well, they'll sure not think we're men of the cloth,' Murdoch answered just as softly. 'But it's the snake-eyed newcomer we have to fool. The two who've been tailin' us ain't got the brains to be anything other than cattle-lifters or bushwhackers, but their buddy is as bad as they come. That makes it he must be a cunnin' sonuvabitch to have stayed alive as long as he has.'

'I think you're dead right, Murdoch,' Skeeter said. 'He has the look of the James boys and you know what mischief they got up to. Now let's haul our asses along to the cathouse. It would give us the chance to see if they think we ain't worth tailin' any more.'

'If we haven't shook them off, what do we do next, Skeeter?' Murdoch asked.

Skeeter gave his partner a fearsome grin. 'Well, I'll just have to throw a scare in them that will have them opinin' that I'm as bloodthirsty as Crazy Horse that day up on the Big Horn when him and his wild boys cut Colonel Custer's troopers into little pieces.' He kicked his chair over with a clatter as he stood up. Swaying unsteadily on his feet he mouthed drunkenly, 'Let's go and get us a woman, pard. And the liquor might be more drinkable in the whore-house. What I've been drinkin' would take the linin' off a swamp 'gator's innards!'

Murdoch grabbed hold of Skeeter's arm to keep him upright. 'All right you drunken sonuvabitch, let's go before you get us thrown out into the street for causin' a disturbance.'

Murdoch, holding on to a make-believe drunken, dirty-mouthing Skeeter, still managed to cast wary-eyed glances over his shoulder as they made their way along the boardwalk to the cathouse. And had his fears justified, and did some cursing of his own. 'That *hombre* who was at the livery barn is doggin' us, Skeeter,' he growled. 'You better do your act or the sonuvabitch could be watchin' us peformin' in the whorehouse.'

It was dark now and Bub temporarily lost sight of the men he was trailing. A puzzled frown creased his brow when, by the light of a lantern hanging on the porch of a store, he could only see one of them. The little drunk had vanished. Maybe, Bub thought, the big man had got tired of lugging his partner around and dumped him on the boardwalk. He would have to watch his step in case he stumbled over him. Bub stepped carefully across the dark opening of an alley, and found the little drunk.

Bub couldn't see him but he felt his arm round his throat, yanking his head back savagely, knocking his hat off, and the son-of-a-bitch's big knife sawing away at the skin of his forehead. His fearful scream echoed along Main Street as he struggled frantically to break out the iron grip before he was scalped, pissing his pants at the same time.

Murdoch hurried back along the boardwalk and pulled Skeeter away from Bub. 'You can't go scalpin' white-eyes, Skeeter!' he said. 'Crows, Blackfeet and the throat-cuttin' Sioux, yeah, but not white men.'

Bub sagged back against the store wall feeling the pain of the long gash and the stickiness of blood on his brow. He wanted to get out of the murderous asshole's clutches, kicking and struggling in his partner's arms, waving the blood-chilling knife in front of his nose, but his fear-numbed brain couldn't get his legs to move.

'The bastard has been trailin' us since we hit town, Murdoch!' Skeeter cried. 'He's after stealin' our gold. He ain't nothin' but a common thief. I've got every right to lift his hair!'

'The law here could think otherwise, Skeeter,' replied Murdoch. 'And I told you in the saloon that we want no trouble with the marshal. So just let him be; I reckon you've scared him enough to keep him off our backs till we leave town. Now just calm down, Skeeter, or you'll be no good to those purty girls in the whorehouse.' He looked at Bub. 'Pilgrim,' he said, 'I'd forget that foolish notion of stealin' our pokes. The few ounces of gold we've collected ain't worth havin' your hair lifted, believe me. As you've found out, my pard is more than somewhat unstable when liquored up. You get back to the saloon and your drinkin', and think on this: if I wasn't such a charitable-minded man you'd be bald by now.'

The frantic messages from Bub's brain finally got through to his legs. Cursing and sobbing, he pushed his way past Murdoch and Skeeter and in a stumbling run made for the safety of the Long Branch.

Murdoch grinned at Skeeter as he let go of him. 'I swear you put on an act that the late John Wilkes Booth in his heyday couldn't have bettered.' He paused, narrow-eying Skeeter. 'You didn't really intend scalpin' that pilgrim, did you, pard?'

'To be truthful, Murdoch, I almost got carried away. Do you think I've Injun blood in me?'

'I dunno about that, Skeeter,' replied Murdoch. 'But I must admit you always were a sneaky sonuvabitch. I reckon I won't be so comfortable sleepin' at the same fire as you in case I wake up bald-headed.'

'A small price to pay, pard, for gettin' the Slash Y snoopers off our tails,' Skeeter said. 'Now let's go and buy us some time with a coupla hot-blooded females.'

Bub almost fell through the doors of the Long Branch.

'Jesus H. Christ!' Slats gasped, jerking upright in his chair on seeing Bub's blood-smeared face. 'Have you ran into a wall?' he asked as Bub flung himself down in a chair.

Bub wiped the blood from his eyes with his bandanna and glared wild-eyed at Clanton. 'I've been almost scalped!' The words came out fast and hysterical. 'Those two sonsuvbitches ain't regulators, they're a coupla crazy hill-billies! The little drunk thought I was after his gold. The bastard went for me with his knife. If his pard hadn't pulled him off me I would've been lyin' back in that alley with no hair! I ain't goin' within grabbin' distance of them for you, Clanton, or Mr Surtees. If he still wants to find out if they're regulators he can damn well check 'em out himself!' Savagely, Bub took hold of the whiskey bottle and took several mouthfuls of the nerve-steadying liquor.

Clanton had done some terrible things in his life as one of 'Bloody' Bill Anderson's black flag boys: burnt down Free Staters' shacks while the families were still in them; shot men in the back from ambush, but he had never scalped any man, white, red or brown, nor had any of the hard men he rode alongside. Bub must be right: the pair could only be backwoods gold-seekers. Which didn't solve his or Surtees's problem. The bastard regulators were out there someplace, he could smell them.

'OK, Bub,' he said. 'I reckon they're no threat to us, we'll leave them be. We'll spread the net wider. I'll get some more of the boys out tomorrow to check on any two, three-man camps close to town. You two can do what you want to do for the rest of the night.' He got to his feet and walked to the door, heading for the cathouse.

A scowling, sore-headed Bub watched him leave. The sonuvabitch was going to enjoy himself with his woman, he thought angrily. The shock of almost being scalped had put all thoughts of suchlike pleasures from his mind. He would be damned lucky if he could sleep. He took another swig of whiskey with hands that still shook.

Five

'Skeeter,' Murdoch growled, bad-temperedly, 'I swear Charlie Goodnight could bed down every one of his hundred thousand Texas cows among these goddamned trees and we wouldn't find a single one of them unless we accidentally trip over 'em.'

'I have to confess, Murdoch,' replied Skeeter. 'I ain't seen as many trees growin' in one place before. On the southern flats a man can see as far as he could ride across in a day. Here, once you leave a so-called trail, you're lost in the timber. We've got more chance of findin' gold, than findin' Fort Whoop-up in these forests.'

Murdoch and Skeeter had spent four fruitless days scouting in the thickly timbered territory along the Montana-Canadian border. They hadn't even come across a single line-trapper's shack let alone a cluster of cabins that could possibly be Fort Whoop-up. They had picked up several tracks of horses and cattle on trails well away from the main border crossings but had lost them when the rustlers had driven the animals across creeks or hard ground. Now, at a night camp, they were taking stock of their progress, or lack of it, in hunting down the rustlers, and deciding their next moves.

'M'be we should head back to Montana, Skeeter,' Murdoch said. 'See if we can pick up a hot trail there that could lead us to Fort Whoop-up.'

'Ritchie and his boys tried that,' Skeeter said. 'But got nowhere.' He grinned at Murdoch across the fire. 'We could ride up to the Slash Y big house and have face-to-face words with Mr Surtees. Accuse him of bein' the brains behind the cattle-liftin' that's goin' on in the territory. Then play it from there.'

Murdoch favoured him with a sour-faced glare. Then suddenly his face hardened, taking on an alert look. 'Or we could have words with that fella tryin' to sneak up on us. Ask him if he knows where Fort Whoop-up is. You just stay on your butt, Skeeter, while I do my own pussy-footin' around.' He got up from the fire and, loud-voiced, said, 'I'll go and check on the horses, pard, before we settle down for the night. Make sure they can't break loose if they get spooked by wolves comin' in close durin' the night, or we'll be stranded among these goddamned trees.'

Constable Pete Slade, Royal Canadian Mounted Police, had dismounted as soon as he had first caught the tangy smell of woodsmoke. Woodsmoke meant a camp, a camp meant men. Men, he hopefully thought, who were stealing horses from the border ranches. He would never find them otherwise. All the tracks of the stolen horses he had trailed had petered out in the vastness of the forest. It would be a meeting where he had the edge of surprise. He gripped his Winchester tighter. A few more yards and he could stop his crawling to walk boldly into the camp as the representative of the Queen's law in the border regions should do and interrogate the men.

Pete heard a man say he was going to see to the horses. He smiled. It was going to be easier than he had thought. It would raise no sweat throwing down on the man left at the fire, then surprise his partner on his return to the camp. Though he was some-what disappointed that he wasn't about to walk in on the horse-stealing gang the two men may know of the location of Fort Whoop-up.

It was Pete who got the surprise, a blood-chilling one. The double snick of a shell being levered into the chamber of a rifle sounded like the bells of Hell in his ears.

'You just leave your rifle lyin' on the ground, mister, and get to your feet, and keep your hands held high.' Pete recognized the voice as belonging to the man who said he was going to see to the horses. Pete got on to his feet, slowly. He had a pistol, in a flapped cavalry holster under his belted mackinaw. It might as well have been in his locker back at the police barracks for what use it was right now.

Murdoch jabbed the rifle in his captive's back, forcibly, as he bent over and picked up the discarded rifle, then raised-voiced, he called out, 'We're comin' in, Skeeter! Everything's OK!' Murdoch's order of,

'Walk, mister, and keep it peaceable,' was accentuated by more sharp, painful thrusts of his rifle.

Once Pete had reached the fire he got his first chance to see his captors and professionally assess them. One was a small man, holding a pistol on him. The man who had jumped him was big and hairy-faced, looking like a grizzly in his ragged fur coat. The most villainous-looking pair of outlaws he had ever come up against, and they had the upper hand. Men, he had no doubts, wanted by the law-enforcing agencies in the States for crimes more serious than mere horse-stealing.

'You open that fancy coat of yours, mister,' Murdoch said. 'And take out that handgun you must be totin' and drop it to the ground, nice and easy-like.'

Pete, silently cursing himself for allowing the big hulk of a man to catch him unawares, did as he was ordered. Not that he lacked courage. He had served arrest warrants on drunk-crazy full-blood Sioux,

French 'breeds, every bit as wild as any Indian when their blood was inflamed by backwoods-stilled rotgut whiskey. It wouldn't be brave to make a grab for his pistol and force a shoot-out, just foolhardy suicidal. The sons-of-bitches would gun him down when the urge took them. There was no sense in bringing that fearful moment forward. He began to unbutton his coat.

It was Skeeter who first glimpsed the red tunic beneath the heavy coat. 'Why, Murdoch!' he said. 'You've brung in a Canadian lawman, and you was thinkin' he was a no-good owlhooter.'

'How the hell was I to know that in the dark,' grumbled Murdoch. 'He sure was sneakin' around like a bad-ass.'

'Yeah, I'm a mountie,' Pete said, surprised and much eased at the sudden uplifting in his fortunes. 'I'm working out White Water Falls police post; name is Pete Slade, Constable Slade.'

Skeeter grinned. 'You'd better sit down and share our chow and coffee, Pete, as a kinda apology for us thinkin' that you had evil intentions towards us. We're a couple of Cattlemen's Association members.'

Pete grinned back at Skeeter. 'To be honest, Mr Skeeter, I opined that law-abiding men wouldn't be camping here in the back of the beyond and took it that more than likely whoever was here could be part of the bunch of horse-thieves I've been trying to track down for the last six months. Or m'be fellas who could be persuaded to guide me to that robbers' roost, Fort Whoop-up.'

'Fort Whoop-up!' Murdoch gasped. 'Well ain't that a coincidence, Skeeter! We're seekin' that place, though we're lookin' for cattle-lifters who are stealin' a Montana rancher's cows. He reckons Fort Whoop-up is where they do their dealin's. But like you, Pete, we ain't found the durn place.'

'We were about to give it up as a bad job,' Skeeter told Pete. 'Reckonin' on trailin' back across to Montana to see if we could be luckier there in pickin' up the rustlers' tracks. Then Murdoch heard you snoopin' around and we thought we had struck gold.'

Pete began to do some rapid thinking. Skeeter and his partner had the cut of men who knew their business. If they could be prevailed upon to stay this side of the border then there would be three of them checking out possible trails leading to Fort Whoop-up. 'If you gents allow me to bring my horses in,' he said, 'I'll have that coffee and grub then we can talk over our problem and see if we can come up with a solution.'

'It sounds fair to us, Constable,' replied Skeeter. 'Me and Murdoch have been goin' round in circles for the last coupla days. Any new ideas on how we can rope in the rustlers will be most welcome.'

'I opine we should ask someone where this Fort Whoop-up is,' Murdoch said. 'Even the three of us ain't goin' to find it, unless we fall over the damn place. I intend quittin' the regulatin' game after this assignment, and I don't want to be too old to enjoy the rockin' chair on the front porch. And it's becomin' to look that way up in these woods. Unless we can get some Injuns to track for us.' Murdoch shot a sharp-eyed glance at the mountie. 'Though I reckon you boys would have done that a while back if it had been possible.'

The three of them had eaten and were sitting around the fire, smoking and drinking their coffee, discussing ways of catching the cattle and horse-rustlers, coming up with nothing new.

'The reason we haven't been able to use Indians for tracking, Mr Murdoch,' Pete said, 'is because the few Indians who trap out here get their liquor from Fort Whoop-up. And because we don't allow Indians to buy whiskey legally, no Indian is going to be so crazy to cut off his supply of firewater. Even any Indian we brought from the Alaskan border.'

'Takin' up your point, Murdoch,' Skeeter said. 'Who the hell do we ask? We ain't met anyone in these woods but the constable here, and he's no wiser than us.'

'Why, back there,' Murdoch replied, jerking a thumb over his shoulder. 'There must be a town of sorts, with a saloon in it. The men who are stealin' the horses and the cattle won't be passin' their free time away livin' in holes in the ground out here. If they're not at Fort Whoop-up they'll be in some town's bar livin' it up with the dollars they've raked in sellin' the stolen stock.'

'There is a settlement, Morgan's Creek, twenty, twenty-five miles clear of the timber south of here,' Pete said. 'It ain't much of a place, but it boasts a bar-cum-bawdy-house. If a man wants anything better to spend his money on he'll have to hard-ass a day's ride further south. Morgan's Creek is frequented by border hard-men.' Pete smiled. 'I've had occasion to ride into the place and arrest wanted men. But I can't see any of them talking to a redcoat, or to Yankee strangers asking nosy questions.' He smiled again. 'More than likely it'll be my duty to go in and arrest your killer.'

'But they might open their tight-shut lips to a coupla horse-thieves,' Murdoch said, 'who are lookin' for a buyer for some horses that have just happened to come their way. Of course, me and Skeeter will have to get us some horses.' He favoured Pete with an all-toothed beaming smile. 'Do you reckon me and my pard will pass as no-good horse-thieves, Constable?'

'Mr Murdoch,' replied Pete, blank-faced, 'no offence intended, but you two would pass for a pair of genuine grandmother throat-cutters. As for horses, well, we have a string of remounts at the post. M'be, just m'be, I could persuade my inspector to let you "borrow" them. But you'll have to ride in with me to back me up.' What was more likely the inspector would open up the cell doors, Pete thought, thinking he was bringing in two notorious outlaws. 'It's a way-out chance the inspector agreeing to fall in with our scheme, but no more way out as the three of us stumbling through these trees and suddenly finding Fort

Whoop-up, or a bunch of horse-thieves.'

Murdoch grinned at Pete. 'If your inspector OKs the plan you'll have two more rustlers in your territory. Now that's enough jawin', we want an early start in the morning to get things rollin'. Me and Skeeter don't want Mr Ritchie firin' off wires to our boss complainin' he ain't payin' out hard cash for agents, who he opines, are sittin' on their butts doin' damn all to stop his cows bein' stolen. You take the first watch, Skeeter; wake me for the second shift. Good night, *compadres.*' Then he stretched himself out on his blanket.

Six

Once they had cleared the timberline the land began to level out in lush green, well-watered terrain. They were riding at a steady pace along a regular trail which Pete told them would see them reaching Morgan's Creek within the hour.

'Across the line,' Skeeter said, 'this piece of real estate would be crawlin' with cattle.'

'It's too close to the border, Mr Skeeter,' replied Pete. 'Cattle grazing here would be an open invitation for Yankee rustlers to cut out a few head and drive them over the Montana border before the rancher knew he had lost any cows. Though there is a small horse ranch away to our left owned by a Mr Doug Pevril. He's an ornery old goat who reckons him and his two grandsons could beat off any attempt by no-good Yankee sons-of-bitches, or any other sons-of-bitches, his very words, Mr Skeeter, to try and steal his stock.'

Both Skeeter and Murdoch looked across to their left and in the far distance saw a thin column of smoke from a ranch-house chimney reaching into the big blue globe of a sky. Then they heard the faint rattle of gunfire.

Pete's face hardened. 'Sounds if old man

Pevril is having trouble.' He began to unloosen his mackinaw. 'I'll have to ride across there and check it out. If Pevril sees my coat he'll know I'm friendly and not shoot at me. There's no need for you boys to come, you ain't Canadian lawmen.'

'Some of the shootin' could be comin' from those horse-thieves you're huntin', Constable,' Skeeter said. 'If they are and we can catch one of them alive and make him talk I'm bettin' on him givin' us a lead to the fellas me and Murdoch are bein' hired to bring in. Or at least point us in the direction of Fort Whoop-up. So it's in our best interests for us to ride with you. And, accordin' to all the firin' I'm hearin' it seems a lot of guns for you, Pevril, and his boys to take on.'

Pete didn't show his relief in his face at Skeeter's willingness to help. He had hoped the two Yankee manhunters would back him up, but his pride in being a mountie wouldn't allow him to ask for help from anyone outside the service.

'But keep that red coat of yours covered up,' Murdoch said. 'Me and my pard don't want to be seen in cahoots with the local law. It'll blow our cover.' He beady-eyed Pete. 'And we go in sneakylike. Me and Skeeter ain't a couple wild-assed Glory boys.'

Jules Brown Bear was doing a whole lot of cursing. He knew now why Purvis hadn't raided the ranch, the nearest to the border before. And with only an old man and two boys to defend it. Kids they may be, he thought angrily, but their shooting was as deadly accurate as any man who fancied himself as an expert with a long gun. Two of his men lying in crumpled heaps in front of the horse corral were stark testimony to their ability to shoot.

It was his first raid since taking over as boss of the gang and he was well aware that it would be his last if he got any more of the gang killed and no horses to show for it. And that would happen if the six of them made a wild dash for the horses. The three rifles, two firing at them from the shack, and one firing at them from the big barn would kill them all dead before they had covered a couple of yards of ground from the ditch they were eating dirt in.

If by some miracle they did make it to the horses, still on their feet, the animals, kicking and rearing, spooked by all the shooting, would stampede in all directions once the corral gate retaining bars were lifted. Somehow the three rifles had to be put out of action. He had foolishly got Dodds and Fletch killed by believing that coming in on the ranch at first light the occupants would still be asleep. And so it had looked, with window shutters still closed and no sign or sound of movement inside or outside the shack. If it hadn't been for the smoke coming out of the stack the ranch could be taken as being deserted.

Instead of sending a man in to check on the barn and other outbuildings, he had sent Fletch and Dodds, mounted up, to act as herders when he and the rest of the gang on foot went into the corral to lead out the horses. A rapid fusillade of shots from the barn cleared Dodds and Fletch out of their saddles. The rest of them managed to reach the shelter of a ditch that ran across the front of the shack just as two more rifles opened up on them from the loopholes in the shack's window shutters.

To roust the gang into staying and make a fight of it after all the losses being on their side was asking for a bullet in his back. Brown Bear knew he had to take that chance, reasoning as his pa's blood kin would in a suchlike situation that death was preferable to loss of face by being rejected by his men as their leader.

Crazy-eyed, he snarled, 'I ain't leavin' the horses! Even if it means puttin' the torch to everything that will burn on this god-damned place to get them. I ain't goin' to let an old man and two snot-nosed kids crow about how they beat off a bunch of horse-thieves and shot down two of them. If you boys ain't got the stomach for a fight then

I'll take on the sonsuvbitches myself, kinda even up the score for Dodds and Fletch.' Brown Bear wasn't shedding any tears for Dodds and Fletch but to protect his ass he had to show concern for the loss of two of his boys.

Wade, the man who had fancied taking over the gang after Purvis had been killed, cast a quick glance at the other four members of the gang, getting slight head nods from them all in return; then he looked back at Brown Bear. He gave a gap-toothed grimace of a smile. 'The boys ain't seen a good fire since the last July the Fourth.'

Brown Bear's smile matched his in fierceness. 'We'll do it like this then.'

Pevril smiled encouragingly across the room at his grandson, Harvey. 'Your brother is sure givin' the thievin' sonsuvbitches something to ponder over. And now we've got them pinned down too scared to show their faces.' He gave Harvey's mother and grandmother, busy in the far corner of the room thumbing reload shells into the magazines of two spare rifles, the same reassuring smile. He opined they were well forted up, the thick timber planking of the walls and shutters a firm barrier against the rustlers' fire.

Though Pevril was worried about Jim, his oldest grandson, out there on his ownsome in the big barn. He was the weak link in the defence of the ranch, the one in the most danger. If the raiders decided to rush the barn the boy would have no chance of holding them off, he would be overrun and killed. Yet if Jim hadn't been in the barn all night waiting for a mare to foal, he would have lost all his stock. His firing had given them in the shack a few minutes' warning, long enough for him and Harvey to get to the loopholes, still in their night clothes, and open fire on the raiders.

He was hoping the killing of two of the gang would deter them from carrying on with the raid. Till he saw them pulling back to where he reckoned they had tethered their horses, they would have to stay at hair-trigger alertness. 'You cover the barn, Harvey,' he said. 'Drop any man who tries to rush Jim, OK?'

'OK,' replied Harvey, peering cautiously through the shutter's firing slot.

While two of the gang kept on firing at the shack and the barn, Brown Bear and the rest of them belly-crawled their way along the ditch till they were covered from the deadly handled rifles by a dip in the ground. Then, moving left, climbed up a narrow ridge and the high ground above the shack, from where, Brown Bear calculated, the soddy-roofed building would be in easy throwing distance of flaming torches; and a good spot to gun down everyone who rushed out of the shack to escape a roasting.

Pevril began to wonder why there were only two rifles firing at them. It didn't take long for him to figure it out. With blood-chilling certainty he knew what devilry the rest of the gang were about to inflict on him and his family. His high hopes of the gang losing two men would call it a day had been dashed. He would rather have all his horses taken than see his family burnt out and shot down like dogs. Pevril ground his teeth in barely suppressed rage. And he had faithfully promised his son as he lay on his death bed he would take care of the two boys and their mother.

Not wishing to alarm the womenfolk, and Harvey, he said, as casually as he could, 'You keep an eye on the barn as I told you, Harvey. I'll watch out back in case them fellas who ain't firin' are tryin' to sneak up on us by the back way.'

Leaving their horses tethered in a hollow behind them, Murdoch, Skeeter and Constable Slade slithered over the crest as low down as three sidewinders. Below them they had a clear view of the shack and the flashes of the raiders' rifles.

'There's two pieces firin' from the shack, and another from that big barn,' Murdoch said. 'It looks as though the old man and his boys are still OK, Pete.'

'Thank God for that, Mr Murdoch,'

replied Pete. 'Old Pevril dotes on his grandsons since his son died. And I can see what looks like two bodies lying in front of the corral.' He grinned at Murdoch and Skeeter. 'Those bastards have found out the hard way that Doug Pevril and his boys are handy with their guns. Counting the two firing from the ditch that makes four rustlers, not a big enough gang to move all those horses in the corral there fast to where they're taking them.' The mountie's face twisted in puzzlement. 'We heard a damn sight more guns; where the hell are the rest of the sonsuvbitches?'

'There they are,' Skeeter said. He pointed to his left. 'Just comin' into the clear between us and the shack.'

'I see them,' said a stone-faced Pete. 'The murdering bastards, they're set on burning down the shack and there's women inside!'

'I reckon getting two of their *amigos* shot dead has kinda raised up their blood somewhat,' Murdoch said. He favoured Pete with one of his beaming, soulless smiles. 'I opine it's time we upset those *hombres* down there a mite further. We ain't got time to get any closer to them – they're almost set to throw those torches – so spread out and start shootin'.'

The first Brown Bear knew his luck was still running bad for him was seeing Blackie, hand drawn back ready to throw the first torch, spin round and drop heavily to the ground without so much as a cry or even a groan. His body rolled a few paces down the slope before bouncing up against a rock that stopped its descent. A split-second later, Brown Bear heard the echoing crack of the shot that had torn a bloody, fist-sized exit hole in Blackie's chest.

Then came the hair-raising scream of a man hit low down, fatally, leaving only him and Bret to burn down the shack, which in the process of being picked off by riflemen above them, meant that they had no time to start the fire if they didn't want to end up quick dead like Blackie or the painfully limb-thrashing, dying Chillis.

Brown Bear flung down his torch and set off in crouching, weaving run back to the flats, physically cringing as shells hissed ominously close to his ears, or raised spurts of dust at his feet. He heard Bret's laboured breathing ending suddenly in a choking gasp, then he was no longer running at his heels. Brown Bear dirty-mouthed. In a matter of seconds he had all but lost his gang. He cut across the slope, heading straight for the horses, Dutch and Casper down there in the ditch, would have to fend for themselves. It was looking out for number-one time.

The burst of gunfire from the ridge puzzled Pevril at first. It seemed to be long ways from where he opined the raiders would be able to fling torches on to the roof of the shack. Had he misread their intentions? The slope at the back of the house was too steep for him to see just what the raiders were up to without stepping outside, and he didn't want to take that risk. And as yet he hadn't seen any tell-tale wisps of smoke seeping through the ceiling planking that would herald the beginning of a fight to the death, the deaths of the Pevril clan.

Then a slow smile broke up the grim lines in his face. It wasn't going to be such a one-sided fight after all, they had allies. It could only be Constable Slade, he thought, though the mountie worked this stretch of the territory on his own and he could hear more than one rifle in action. Whoever they were he was beholden to them. He walked back into the living-room all smiles.

'It's goin' to be OK, folks,' he said. 'It sounds as though some good Samaritans are up on the back ridge helpin' us out. But we can't drop our guard till the last of the raiders are dead, or we see them hightail it out of here.'

Dutch and Casper could see the small massacre taking place on the high ground, and the fleeing figure of their boss leaving them to take on six rifles.

'The dirty stinkin' 'breed's got four of the

boys killed, now he's chickenin' out on us!'
Dutch cried. 'There's no reason for us to
stay and get plugged; we ain't goin' to get
any horses on this raid that's for sure. Let's
get the hell outa it! And I swear if I ever
meet up with that part Injun I'll gut-shoot
him for pullin' out on us! You cover me,
Casper, till I get clear, then I'll do likewise
for you from back there, OK?' Without
waiting for Casper's agreement, Dutch
began scrambling out of the ditch. And
Harvey killed his first man. Dutch fell back
into the ditch hit by a shot that had
shattered his head into bloody pieces.

A pinch-faced Casper didn't want anyone
digging a grave for him. He tossed his rifle
then his pistol clear of the ditch yelling,
'There's only me down here and I'm
quittin'! I'm comin' with my hands held
high so don't shoot!'

'You come out nice and easy-like, mister!'
Jim called out from the barn. 'Or you're
dead for sure!' He sounded more confident
than he was feeling. He had thrown up after

he had killed the two raiders. He took a sighting along his rifle. Guts heaving or not, they were relying on him back in the house.

Pevril grinned at Harvey, both of them had heard the rustler's shout of surrender. 'It looks as though we're goin' to win this war. You and Jim have done well. Keep that fella comin' out of the ditch covered till we know for certain he's had his bellyful of fightin'. I'll go out back to see how things are developin' up on the ridge.'

'I do believe one of the raiders is givin' himself up, boys,' Murdoch said, as the three of them got to their feet. 'Pity we can't go down and pass the time of day with him, Skeeter. You could show him that big pigsticker of yours, loosen his tongue somewhat.' He fierce-grinned. 'Could tell us where that robber's roost is located, loud enough for them to hear it in Montana.'

Skeeter noticed the puzzled look on Pete's face at hearing they were not going to interrogate the raider.

'One of those cattle-lifters is still on the

loose, Pete,' he said. 'Now he could be still runnin' scared, but me and Murdoch can't take that as gospel. Bein' natural born suspicious men, men who want to enjoy sittin' in a rocking chair in our old age, we have to suppose that he could be hunkered down hereabouts wantin' to see just who the hell it was who killed two of his buddies and had him runnin' like a scared cat. If he's a mean vindictive *hombre* he'll mark us. And as sure as hell I wouldn't want to meet up with him at Fort Whoop-up among all his friends when we're tryin' to pass ourselves off as border hardcases.'

'We'll come down after dark,' Murdoch said, 'bring all the horses with us. Make sure you keep that raider locked up in one of the barns. And let the Pevrils know we're comin' in. We don't want those sharp-shootin' kids of his to cut loose at us. I ain't the size of target even a poor shot could miss in the dark.'

'It's time I let old man Pevril know that the fighting up here is over; he's just come out of the shack. He'll be wondering just who his friends are.' He fired three shots from his rifle into the air then opened his mackinaw wide to clearly show his red tunic. 'It's me, Constable Slade!' he yelled. 'With some friends! It's all clear up here, so I'm comin' on down!'

Pevril's three shots were his acknowledging OK.

It was full dark when Murdoch and Skeeter rein-leading their horses picked their way down from the ridge. Jim cradling his rifle, was circling the barn, the prison, of the bound-hand-and-foot Casper. His stomach had lost its queasiness over the shooting of the rustlers. He opined Harvey had felt the same way after he had killed his man though he hadn't said so. When his grandpa had told him of the raiders' plan to put a torch to the house, Jim wished he had gunned down more of the sons-of-bitches.

He listened intently for the grating sound of ironshod hooves slipping on loose stones, the noises horses would make being led by men unfamiliar with the ground they were crossing in the dark. He gasped and spun round in alarm at the sound of a deep, gruff voice behind him saying, 'Evening boy. I'm Mr Murdoch. Mr Skeeter is back of me bringin' in the horses. You'll have been told to expect us I reckon.'

Although there was only starlight to break up the darkness, he could see that Mr Murdoch was built like a barn. How had the big man crept up on him so silently? And how the heck had he not heard the horses? Had the big man carried them down from the ridge? He had the size and the strength to do so. Constable Slade had told his grandpa that the two Yankees were the sneakiest pair of men he had ever come across. And they had just proved it by almost making him crap himself

'Yeah, we've been expectin' you,' he said, his nerves settling down, albeit slowly. 'Grandpa told me I had to see to the horses and to tell you to go on inside. Ma's got a meal ready for you both. Oh, Constable Slade said I also had to tell you that the rustler we captured is tied up in the big barn, well out of sight of what's goin' on.'

'Food on the table, boy?' Murdoch said. 'That's the most welcoming news me and Mr Skeeter have heard since crossin' into Canada.'

Jim saw the glinting whiteness of the big man's teeth as he smiled down at him.

'And just for the record, boy,' Murdoch continued, 'you and your brother stood your ground as good as, if not better, than any man. Ain't that so, Skeeter?'

'I couldn't put it any better myself,' replied Skeeter.

A pouting-chested proud Jim had to look really hard in the dark before he picked out the small, slight shape of Mr Murdoch's partner. A man hardly as big as he was.

'Give me the reins, Mr Skeeter,' he said. 'I'll see that the horses are fed and watered. You get yourselves indoors. Ma and Grandma will cause a ruckus if the food is spoilt waitin' for you to show up.'

'Let's do as the boy says, Murdoch,' Skeeter said. 'We ain't strong enough characters to withstand the fury of two females.'

Seven

'The sonuvabitch is tight-lipped,' Pete said. 'Won't even tell me the name of the raider who cut and run for it. So while we've done a good job in wiping out a bunch of horse-thieves, we're no nearer to finding the location of Fort Whoop-up.'

Murdoch, Skeeter and Pete had eaten well and were sitting on the front porch of the cabin, Murdoch and Skeeter trying to figure out the next move to rope in the Montana rustlers on hearing the disappointing news of the non-cooperation of their prisoner. The old rancher and Jim had taken the three raiders killed at the front of the house up on to the ridge to bury them alongside the two shot dead there. Harvey was guarding the prisoner.

'Though I did pick up some information which could be of some help to you gents,' Pete continued. He grinned at the pair. 'The rustler wouldn't talk but one of his buddies' horses as good as talked to me.'

Murdoch and Skeeter stiffened up, puzzle-eyed. 'We're all ears, Pete,' Murdoch said, 'to hear what this talkative critter spoke to you about.'

'It was its tracks that did the talking, Murdoch,' Pete said. 'Two days ago I came across the tracks of a bunch of cows being driven along the main trail from the border. I managed to get a clear reading of some of the trail-hands' horses. One of the horses had a nail missing out of its left hind shoe. That horse is now in the corral over there. Are you beginning to get the picture, friends?'

'Well I'll be damned!' Skeeter exclaimed. 'The sonsuvbitches are runnin' a smooth operation here, Murdoch! Exchangin' stolen Montana cows for horses illegally taken here in Canada. Me and Murdoch have been searchin' for cattle-thieves when we should have been eyeballin' men sellin' horses holdin' Canadian bills of sale, phoney ones, in Montana.'

'And the horse-thieves I've been trying to hunt down,' Pete said, 'have been practically passing me on the trail driving stolen Yankee cattle. The work we did here today cleared up my problem, but it still leaves the boys you two are after on the loose.'

'It's a shame you couldn't get that fella in the barn to talk, Pete,' Skeeter said. 'It looks as though we'll have to try and sweet-talk your boss into giving us those horses after all. Otherwise we ain't goin' to make any progress, ever.' Then he noticed Murdoch's blank-faced, unseeing-eyed expression. 'You're thinkin' up something, pard, ain't you?'

'Sort of,' replied Murdoch, face loosening up.

'Such as?' Skeeter queried.

'Like me and you gettin' real friendly with that rustler,' Murdoch said. 'Make him think that me and you are two genuine Yankee bad-asses.'

'And how do we do that, pard?' Skeeter said, sceptically. 'Pete's goin' to haul him off to jail come daylight. That don't give us a long spell to get pally with him, especially when I need a coupla hours' sleep. And how the hell are we goin' to explain to him how we knew he was in the barn in the first place!'

'We ain't goin' to talk to him, not at first anyway,' Murdoch said. 'At Pete's first night camp along the trail, two Yankee *desperadoes* will burst in on him to steal his horses and gear. Pete will naturally try to stop us from robbin' him. I'll shoot him dead,' Murdoch grinned at Pete. 'Not for real, of course. Then to show how mean I am I make as though I'm about to plug the fella you're takin' in when I suddenly find he's a tied-up prisoner. So I change my

106

mind and release him instead.'

'That kindly act,' Skeeter said, 'oughta make the fella as friendly towards us as a kissin' cousin. M'be loosen his tongue somewhat and tell us where the other wild boys hole-up, such as Fort Whoop-up.' It was Skeeter's turn to grin at Pete. 'You'll have to "die" real good; the rustler mustn't get a smell of it bein' a big con.'

Pete gazed long and hard at Murdoch and Skeeter. How could they come up with such a mad-assed plan, he wondered. He would be kicked out of the Force if his inspector ever found out he had handed a prisoner over to men who weren't legally appointed lawmen, even in the States. Then he had a brief wild thought of his own. Suppose the pair were already doing their conning. They were not regulators but owlhooters. Helping him to kill Pevril's rustlers had been their chance to get rid of their rivals in the trade. The pair, Pete thought, could even be members of the gang they were supposed to be hunting down.

Murdoch, seeing Pete's troubled look, knew what was passing through the mountie's mind. They were asking him to do a lot on trust, lay his job on the line, no less. And he had to admit that his and Skeeter's appearance would raise doubts in any man's mind regarding their honesty and trustworthiness. 'Show Pete our credentials, Skeeter,' he said. 'He don't quite accept we've got halos round our heads.'

Skeeter reached into an inside pocket and drew out an oilskin-covered packet and handed it across to Pete.

Pete gave a dismissive wave of his hand, refusing to take it. 'Ah, hell,' he mumbled, embarrassedly. 'I know you're lawmen it's just that your "sorta plan", Murdoch, kinda threw me for a minute or two, that's all. Though thinking it through it's wild enough to work.' He smiled. 'I'll *die* real fine for you boys. But you'll have to promise me one thing first.'

'Name it!' said Murdoch.

'If you make it to Fort Whoop-up,' Pete

said, 'you burn it down. Put an end to its use as a hole-up for Yankee and Canadian border scum. If you can do that my inspector won't throw me out of the service for backing this plan of yours.'

'We'll do that for you, Pete, with great pleasure,' replied Murdoch. 'It's in the best interests of lawmen both sides of the border to see that robbers' roost closed down.'

Pete had no lingering doubts now that Murdoch and Skeeter were on the side of law and order. He was also convinced they were a couple of mad-brained sons-of-bitches. How else had they stayed so long above ground as regulators?

As befitting their new image as drifters looking for easy pickings, they left the packhorse with the Pevrils. Though not before Skeeter had transferred several sticks of dynamite from the stores to his saddle-bags. He would do more than burn down Fort Whoop-up, he thought, he would blow it clear across the State of Montana.

Eight

Casper sat with his back up against a tree, keen-eying the mountie. Though his hands were cuffed behind him, Casper hadn't given up hope of escaping. There would be another night camp before reaching the jailhouse at White Water Falls mountie station and the red-coated son-of-a-bitch couldn't keep awake, or alert all that time. The breaks would come his way for sure, and he would be ready for them, if he didn't want to do a long stretch in the State Pen.

Once he was free he would head for Fort Whoop-up, where he opined, Brown Bear would be. He was still feeling sore at the 'breed for running out on him and Dutch, but looking at the situation from the 'breed's angle what could he have done to help them out? Stay till he got plugged

110

himself? So Casper decided that when he met up with the 'breed at the fort it wouldn't be calling-out time, for financial reasons.

The 'breed would be able to raise another bunch of men willing to steal horses for a living, if it paid well. On his own he could kiss goodbye to the good times, the drinking, the gambling and the pleasurable services of lewd women the cash the rustling trade procured for him. On his own he would have to eat his horse to stay alive. Casper sat back against the tree, watching, waiting for the mountie to make his first slip-up.

Brown Bear crept in closer to the camp. It had been a wild gamble waiting along the trail in the hope that the mountie patrol hadn't killed Dutch and Casper but would be taking them in as prisoners to White Water Falls. He was in a desperate, reputation-saving situation. A gang of two was better than eating crow in front of the Yankee Clanton, for the second time, by telling him he couldn't come through with his end of the deal having had his gang wiped out by the mounties. He would soon be close enough to find out if his luck since taking over the gang was changing for the better.

Brown Bear knew his luck hadn't swung far in his favour when he saw only one prisoner at the camp, Casper. His disappointment was eased somewhat on noticing he had only one mountie to deal with. He wondered, briefly, where the other two mounties who had cut down his three boys from the high ground were. He placed them either still at the ranch or trying to pick up his trail in the hope it would lead them to Fort Whoop-up. Brown Bear thin-smiled. The dead body of the redcoat and his prisoner vanished would show them that things hadn't gone all their way.

Pete heard the slight crack of a snapping twig and smiled inwardly. It was almost time to put on his 'dying' act. His inner smile froze on seeing the man step into the clearing. By his build it was neither Murdoch nor Skeeter. When, by the light of the fire, he could pick out his night visitor's features Pete felt as though he hadn't smiled for a long time. Well acquainted with Jules Brown Bear's face, printed on wanted flyers for two counts of murder and several of robbery, he grabbed for his rifle, lying at his side.

Brown Bear's hatchet-hewn face twisted in a mirthless grin. 'You'll be dead, Mountie, if you pick up that gun,' he said. 'I've had you covered all the way in.'

Pete stayed his hand and gazed at the black muzzle hole of the rifle held steady on him. He was looking at real death. The 'breed knew they couldn't hang him any higher for another killing marked up against him.

'Now get up off your ass, Redcoat,' Brown Bear ordered, 'and free my buddy. Any foolishness and I'll blow you clear into the brush.'

'The sonuvabitch's cuffed me,' Casper

cried. 'Key's in his right-hand coat pocket!'

Brown Bear stepped closer to Pete and jabbed the rifle in his belly. 'Just reach in and take the key out,' he grated. 'I don't want to have to search for it in all the blood I'll cause to flow if you try anything tricky.'

Pete glared angrily, and helplessly, at the 'breed and did what he was told. He wasn't dead yet though he knew the minutes he had left to live were ticking off fast. Frantically he thought of how he could come up with a miracle of sorts to save his life, and couldn't come up with one. His only chance to escape the 'breed's bullet was Murdoch and Skeeter showing up, not too suddenly so as to cause the 'breed's trigger finger to twitch.

He pulled out the handcuffs key from his pocket and showed it to the 'breed then walked across to his prisoner. He wasn't about to give Brown Bear cause to gun him down any sooner than he intended to. Alive, there was still hope.

Murdoch nudged Skeeter in the ribs with

his elbow. 'Time we introduced ourselves, pard,' he whispered. 'Before that other fella gets loose and we've lost some of our edge over that Indian-faced bastard. Before we have a real dead mountie on our hands.'

The pair had been on the edge of the camp about to walk in on Pete when the 'breed came into view opposite them. Either of them could have gunned down the 'breed but the newcomer dead would have been the end of Murdoch's plan to use Pete's captive as a means of getting into Fort Whoop-up. Killing his buddy wouldn't make him co-operative.

Skeeter slowly, quietly drew back the hammer of his Colt with the heel of his hand. 'I'll come at him from behind,' he said, softly. 'Give me a coupla minutes, then go in like a proddin' man and let them know what we've come for.'

Casper struggled to his feet, cursing at Pete. 'Hurry up and get these blasted cuffs off!' he snarled. 'Then you, sonuvabitch, I'm goin' to gutshoot you!'

'The only shootin' that's goin' to get done around here is from me and my pard.' Murdoch's voice boomed across the clearing. He loomed like some great bear in the flickering light from the fire, his rifle looking like a toy gun in his big hands. 'And it will be *pronto* if those of you who can don't grab air.'

An expressionless-faced Brown Bear slowly inched his rifle round to cover the big intruder, his finger taking up the pressure on the trigger. His stoic mask slipped into one of alarm as a voice behind him said, 'You'd better take heed of Murdoch there, pilgrim. He blows up real wild if any *hombre* goes against his sayso. He scares me sometimes, and I'm his long-time pard. Now just drop your rifle as he says. If he misses you, I sure won't.' Skeeter poked the 'breed in the back with his pistol to make certain that the part-Indian had got the message that making a fight of it wasn't an option for him, if he wanted to stay alive.

Brown Bear's rifle hit the dirt with a

deadened thud. Eyes narrow slits of hate, he raised his hands high.

'Good,' said Murdoch. 'Now step in closer to the other two *hombres* so it will give me a nice tight group to blast away at if any of you tries to pull a fast one. Skeeter, bein' that everything is in hand here, you go and rope in the horses and any gear which could be of use to us.'

'You're a coupla horse-thieves?' Brown Bear said, face twisted in surprise.

Murdoch grinned at him. 'We ain't Bible salesmen, that's for sure, mister. If easy money comes our way, why we take it.'

Brown Bear took a chance and lowered his hands. 'I'm Brown Bear,' he said. 'Me and Casper, the fella with the cuffs on, are in the same line of business. He's' – Brown Bear pointed to Pete – 'a mountie. He was takin' Casper to the White Water Falls mountie station. I was just about to free him when you and your pard got the drop on me. Join up with us and in a few days' time we'll get ourselves thirty, thirty-five horses.'

'Thirty-five head you say,' Murdoch said, face screwed up as though weighing up the 'breed's proposal.

'That's right,' Brown Bear said. 'I almost got my hands on them a day or so ago. But a mountie patrol jumped us, killed all my boys but Casper here.'

'That musta been all the shootin' we heard, Murdoch, remember?' Skeeter said.

'Four of us ain't enough men to push that number of stolen horses along fast,' Murdoch said. 'And me and my pard would need to discuss our cut before we throw in with you, mister.'

'Fair enough,' replied Brown Bear. 'First we'll get rid of the mountie then we'll ride to Fort Whoop-up, it's a tradin' post out there in the hills, and hire us a few more boys. On the trail we can come up with a deal that suits us both, Mr Murdoch.'

'We'll ride with you to Fort Whoop-up,' Murdoch said. 'And if we like what you're willin' to pay us, and the boys you're 'tendin' to hire know their business, then I reckon me and Skeeter will help you to steal those horses. Skeeter, put up your pistol and allow Mr Brown Bear to free our new buddy, Mr Casper.'

Casper rubbed his chafed wrists for several seconds after the cuffs had been removed, then cursing loudly, he ripped open Pete's mackinaw and grabbed for his pistol in the flapped holster belted on his right hip. 'I'll get rid of the sonuvabitch!' he snarled.

Murdoch swung round his rifle and knocked Casper's hands away, savage enough for him to yelp, dog-like, with pain, and curse more colourfully.

'What the hell did you do that for?' Casper gasped angrily.

'To save us all from a hangin' or bein' shot dead,' Murdoch said. 'Have you thought where the rest of the mountie patrol who shot your buddies down could be, Casper, eh? They could still be close enough to hear a pistol shot and could come ballin' in here shootin' every which way. Me and Mr

Skeeter ain't *hombres* who take a likin' to ridin' alongside men who don't think carefully and coolly, Skeeter, take that mountie well into the brush before you use your knife on him. We don't want his body found till we've got our cut of the horses we're goin' to lift and back across the line into Montana.'

Skeeter herded Pete into the thickest of the patches of brush with the point of his knife. Once out of sight of the camp, Pete told him all he knew about Brown Bear.

'Watch your backs with the 'breed, Skeeter,' he said. 'He's a killer, twice over. He was second-in-line to another mean-ass called Purvis. Now it looks, for some reason or another, as if the 'breed's taken over the gang.' He smiled. 'Only to lose it at Pevril's ranch.'

'We'll take care, Pete,' replied Skeeter. 'When the 'breed goes for Pevril's horses again, we'll be ridin' with him so warn Pevril not to put up a fight, unless he's pushed into one. Me and Murdoch will do our best to make sure there'll be no shootin' on our side. Tell him not to worry about his horses, we could only be borrowin' them. If he don't get them back we'll see he gets full payment for them. Once we get the horses they'll be the bait to draw the fellas we're huntin' to Fort Whoop-up. Then it'll be up to me and Murdoch to earn our pay.'

Pete was thinking that the Yankees' plans were becoming wilder. Not only would he get kicked out of the Force, the inspector would throw him in jail for aiding and abetting outlaws. Then there was the added problem of sweet-talking old man Pevril to part peaceably with his horses. It would save him a whole heap of trouble and worry, Pete thought morbidly, if Skeeter stuck the knife in him for real.

'I can see what I've just related ain't settlin' easy on your mind, Pete,' Skeeter said. 'But you'll just have to trust us to pull it off, *amigo*; we're supposed to be good in suchlike situations. This is the only way we can play the cards that's been dealt us. To cheer you up I'll promise you this, Pete: if things fall right for us we'll blow up Fort Whoop-up for you. You have my solemn word on it.'

'Yeah, well, you and Murdoch's plans are kinda overwhelming that's a fact,' Pete said. 'We backwoods hicks don't think so big, but I wish you all the luck you'll need to win through.' He was thinking the pair would require all the luck in the world, and then some for their scheme to be successful. 'I'll try and swing Pevril round to your way of thinking, Skeeter, though I'm not promising he'll buy it.'

'You can only do your best, Pete, that's good enough for me,' Skeeter said. 'Then, and I know you won't like it, you get to hell outa this neck of the woods, OK? You're supposed to be dead. The 'breed and Casper don't believe in miracles. If they see you, me and Murdoch are dead meat.'

'Skeeter,' Pete said, soberly, 'The more I dwell on your plan, the more snags I see in it, and I don't intend adding to them. I'll keep my head down, though it goes against the grain to do so.' He shook Skeeter's hand and again wished him and Murdoch the best of luck.

Skeeter walked back into the camp, wiping his knife on a tuft of grass. He shot a sour-faced look at Casper before saying, 'It's done, Brown Bear, now let's go and earn ourselves some spendin' money.'

'Good,' said Brown Bear. 'Get mounted then. We'll make it to the fort by mornin' if we ride hard.'

Murdoch and Skeeter exchanged slight smiles. The trail was hotting up at last. All they had to do was to stay alive, and to shoot faster and truer when the time came than the men they were after.

Nine

Surtees was sitting in his den, chewing savagely at the end of his cigar, too preoccupied with the worry of where the Cattlemen's Protective Association agent, or agents, could be hiding out to light up the Havana.

Time which could have been spent lifting other ranchers' cattle was being wasted by Clanton and his crew checking out abandoned line cabins and trappers' shacks on the off chance they were being used by the regulators. If they weren't eating and sleeping in Red Butte, he knew no strangers to the town had contacted Ritchie, or his woman who ran the rooming-house, they must be somewhere nearby. He didn't doubt they were in the territory.

The cunning bastards would be watching

every night rider moving along the back trails so attempting to steal cattle would be that extra bit dangerous, though Clanton and the hired hands would have to take that risk or the 'breed across in Canada would get to thinking that the deal he had made with him was off. Then the son-of-bitch could ride across the border and set up his own cattle-lifting business here in Montana.

With a disgruntled growl he threw the soggy-ended cigar into the fireplace and got to his feet. He gave a ghost of a smile. It would cheer him up somewhat if Clanton could lift a bunch of Ritchie's cows. It would be like spitting in the bastard's face.

Ritchie was also having unsettling thoughts. Like he was throwing away good money hiring Murdoch and Skeeter, rated as the top regulators in the Association. He was cooling off after a heavy session with Meg Johnson in her private quarters in the rooming-house. He hadn't seen hide nor hair of the pair since their first meeting at the big bluff. Neither had they tried to make contact with him through Meg to let him know what progress they were making in tracking down the rustlers. Bremen, he knew, didn't rank Murdoch and Skeeter very high. Thought he had been foolish to hire them, though he hadn't told him so.

Meg, getting dressed, saw Ritchie's worried face. 'Trouble, honey?' she asked.

'Naw,' Ritchie replied. 'I was just wondering why I ain't heard from those two regulators. When I first saw the pair I admit I got the impression they were men who knew their business, now I ain't so sure. Being that their boss spoke highly of them I was expecting results *pronto* concerning the sonsuvbitches who are stealing my cattle.'

'Jeb,' Meg said. 'I knew of Mr Murdoch's and Mr Skeeter's rep when they were running down rustlers below the Red in Texas. They're the best, believe me. Just give them time to prove it to you. After all, no rancher has lost any cattle since they came into the territory, have they? So it looks as though the rustlers got news of their coming and got scared off.' And that was as far as Meg was willing to tell Ritchie about Murdoch and Skeeter's firm conviction that Surtees and his Slash Y crew were doing the cattle-lifting.

'Yeah, I suppose I'm worrying for nothing, Meg,' replied Ritchie, swinging out of the bed and putting on his pants and boots. He grinned at Meg. 'Wherever they are they're sure not wasting my money drinking and whoring in town.'

From her window Meg watched the rancher cross the street to the mayor's office for his usual weekly game of poker with the town's notables. Then she saw two of the Slash Y crew come staggering out of the Long Branch saloon, the men who had been watching her place when Murdoch and Skeeter paid her a call. They had a companion with them, a pinched-faced man, a stranger to Red Butte. But not to her. Monte Lassiter was the last man she had expected to see in Red Butte. He knew she had been a cathouse madam. Fear pangs clawed at the pit of her stomach, he also knew Murdoch and Skeeter were regulators.

The pair holding warrants on him for cattle-stealing had caught up with Monte in her cathouse. Meg's face steeled over in anger. The gun-crazy son-of-a-bitch had shot his way out of the place, used one of her girls as a hostage to make his escape. Would have killed her too if Murdoch and Skeeter hadn't let him ride out. If she wanted proof that Surtees's men were doing the rustling she was seeing it now. The three of them were talking as though they were old buddies. It seemed that Lassiter was about to take up his cattle-thieving ways here in Montana and could become a deadly threat to Murdoch and Skeeter.

She would have to keep a sharp lookout for the pair showing up to warn them of Lassiter's presence in the territory or their cover would be blown and Clanton's hard men would gun them down. She wondered if she should let Ritchie know that the Slash

Y were hiring notorious cattle-lifters but decided against it. Surtees would naturally deny he knew that his new hand was a wanted man. Ritchie could read it another way, and what Murdoch had warned her about, a killing range war, could break out in Montana.

Her good days in Red Butte were over if Lassiter caught sight of her. He would spread it all over town what her former profession had been. Or demand his way with her for free to keep his mouth shut. Meg's lips thinned into two hard determined lines. Whatever, it would be a price worth paying if she could forewarn Murdoch and Skeeter of the threat against them. She owed them that for preventing more girls from being hurt by Lassiter.

Lassiter had high-tailed it northwards after his near capture by Murdoch and Skeeter. He didn't hanker getting any closer to being shot dead or strung up. That fear had kept him moving fast across the Nations, only pausing long enough to snatch a few hours' sleep or a quick meal. In Colorado, feeling the pressure of the hunt off him, he sought casual work as an odd job hand on ranches there, then later in Wyoming, till finally he ended up in Red Butte, Montana.

Slats and Bub, still on duty checking out strangers coming in, saw him walk into the Long Branch saloon. Bub looked hopefully at Slats. 'I ain't seen him in town before, Slats. Could he be a regulator?'

Slats grinned at him. 'If the regulators got their hands on him he'd swing as high as me and you would. He's an old buddy of mine. Way back him and me were part of a gang of Texas cattle-lifters. I thought old Monte Lassiter would have been took by the Texas Rangers by now. Let's go in and have a drink with him. See what grief caused him to haul ass all this way north.'

Lassiter stiffened up at the bar in surprise on hearing his name being called by one of the two men who had just bellied up to the bar. 'Well I'll be damned!' he exclaimed.

'Slats Wilson! I figured you had ended up dancin' on the end of a rope a long time ago.'

'It's funny, Monte,' Slats said, 'I was thinkin' the same thoughts about you. This is my buddy, Bub. Now tell me what you've been doin' since the gang was broken up.'

Over drinks, Lassiter told Slats and Bub what with being harried by Texas Rangers, marshals' hanging posses and regulators, cattle-lifting in Texas and the Nations was becoming a hazardous trade to follow. Lassiter smiled, drunkenly. 'Though I've second thoughts about that now. Workin' your stones off as a dollar and three-squares-a-day ranch hand ain't a way of life at all for an *hombre* who has strong ambitions to get his hand on some real amounts of foldin' money fast.' Lassiter gave the pair a speculative look. 'Are you boys nursin' cows?' he asked.

Slats and Bub grinned at each other. 'Well, it ain't what you'd call regular ranch work me and Bub do, Monte,' Slats said. 'It's kinda like what me and you were doin' down there in Texas in the old days. Without raisin' as much sweat.'

Lassiter cast a furtive glance around him to see if any other drinker was within earshot before he spoke. 'I've hard-assed all the way here from Texas to find the first two men I meet are in the same line of business as myself. Slats, it must be fate. Your boss won't object to hirin' another hand, will he? My credentials are first class, you know that, Slats.'

Slats glanced into the bar mirror and saw Clanton pushing his way through the swing doors. 'You're in luck, Monte, he's here.' He waved for Clanton to come over and join them. Once at the bar he introduced him to Monte. 'We once rode together in Butch Loagon's gang, Tod,' he continued. 'Now the gang's bust up, Monte was wonderin' if you'd take him on.' Then, not to show Clanton he had been loose-mouthing off about their cattle-lifting activities he said, 'Monte kinda guessed I must still be in the rustlin' business. He couldn't believe I was a thirty-dollar-a-month ranch hand.'

Clanton had heard of the Butch Loagon gang. Hard-riding, wild-shooting boys till the Texas Rangers surprised them in their hole-up in Bull Run canyon and downed Butch and most of the gang for ever. Lassiter, a shut-faced man, and a man who had ridden with the best, was always an asset to any organization. More so in a business where slow shooting could be the difference between living or dying. He reached out a hand. 'Any boys of old Butch's is welcome in my outfit, Monte,' he said. 'I'll have to clear it with the man in the big house, but he should give his OK. Stay here with Slats and Bub, they'll put you wise on how we do things in Montana.' He grinned at Lassiter. 'One thing's for sure, Monte, you won't have Texas Rangers breathin' down your neck up here. Though we've heard there are some regulators snoopin' around, but we'll soon put paid to them. You bring him back to the ranch,

Slats, when you've had your fill. I'll see you all there.' Then he strode out of the saloon before Lassiter could mention how two regulators had almost put paid to him.

What the hell, Lassiter thought, the regulators here in Montana couldn't be as dogged in trailing a man as Murdoch and Skeeter were, and besides they worked out of Fort Smith, Arkansas long ways from here. Smiling at Slats and Bub, he said, 'Let's drink up, boys. I feel like celebratin'. I thought I was goin' to end up nursin' cows or diggin' dirt as a ragged-Levi sodbuster!'

Ten

They had made it to the fort just after daybreak, along a trail that sometimes narrowed to a leafy, dark tunnel beneath low-branched, close-growing timber which forced them down across their horses' necks to prevent them from being swept out of their saddles. With the trail climbing, dropping, twisting this way and that way, Murdoch nor Skeeter knew in which direction Fort Whoop-up lay.

Though Murdoch knew Brown Bear was a killer and a horse-thief and would gladly shoot him dead, or hang him, when the time came, the part-Indian was the best trail reader he had ever met up with. If they brought the stolen stock this way he could understand the lawmen not being able to back track them to the fort.

They had slept for a few hours in an empty shack, Murdoch only fitfully as he tried to work out a plan that would guarantee the Pevrils' safety during the raid. By the time it came to eat he reckoned he had a glimmering of a plan. A plan to be successful, had to rely on other parties playing things how he figured they would – and Skeeter's OK, being as he was to play the main part in his scheme. First, though, he needed some private time to talk it over with Skeeter.

Later in the morning, Murdoch got that privacy. He told Brown Bear that he and Skeeter were going to check out their mounts. He gave the 'breed one of his fearsome smiles. 'If we run into trouble on this caper, me and my pard don't want be ridin' in yours and the boys' trail dust. We want to be ass-kickin' it right alongside you.'

'Yeah, OK, then,' Brown Bear said. 'But don't be too long over it. As soon as Casper and me round up some boys we're movin' out. I want to catch that sonuvabitch rancher with his pants down. He'll not expect another bunch of horse-thieves to show up on his front porch so soon.'

Once at the horse lines, a dip in the ground on the eastern rim of the camp, Skeeter came straight to the point.

'The blasted 'breed's movin' fast, Murdoch,' he said. 'Have you come up with something yet that gets us the horses without old man Pevril and his kin comin' to any harm? Even if Pevril is willin' to co-operate

136

with us we can't just go up to him and ask him to hand over his stock. We've got to keep the 'breed thinkin' we're a coupla bad-assed horsethieves or we're dead.'

'I've been workin' on a plan real hard, Skeeter,' replied Murdoch. 'Most of the blasted night in fact.' He then told Skeeter how he wanted things to go on the raid. Then he asked Skeeter if he thought it could work.

Skeeter gave Murdoch a sidelong glance as he was examining his saddle straps. 'We'll have no trouble at all in pleasin' Pete,' he said. 'I've enough dynamite in my saddle-bags to blow this place to Hell and beyond, along with the no-good killers and thieves who use it as a hole-up. But your plan, well it's kinda dodgy. Though to tell you the truth I sure can't think of a better one right now.'

'Well, since we're bein' honest with each other,' Murdoch said, 'I don't think much of my scheme either. The 'breed ain't the easiest of characters to be told how they should do things. So you act kinda surprised when I suggest to him how I think we should take the horses. I want it to look as though I've just come up with the idea. Then, I hope, he won't think it's a conspiracy between us two to impress the Fort Whoop-up boys that we can pull off better organized raids, and less dangerous, so they'll want us to boss the gang. OK?'

'OK by me, pard,' replied Skeeter.

Murdoch's face stoned over. 'If old man Pevril won't play his part, or Brown Bear don't see eye to eye with me and wants to go fireballin' in, then we start shootin' to kill. No harm must come to the Pevrils, that's our priority. To hell with Ritchie's cattle-lifters.'

Skeeter grinned. 'Take that attitude, Murdoch,' he said, 'and we could be tendin' sheep a heap sooner than we reckoned. Now let's go and tell the boss we're ready to move out on his sayso. There's no need to upset the sonuvabitch before you have to, Murdoch.'

There was still plenty of light left in the day when they, seven of them now, were within sighting distance of the Pevril ranch. A ride, though made in daylight, still didn't make it any easier for Murdoch and Skeeter to think they could find their way back to Fort Whoop-up on their own. Murdoch whispered his doubts to Skeeter when they had dismounted to relieve themselves.

'Skeeter,' he said, 'we'd better not fall out with our new buddies or we'll never blow up Fort Whoop-up; we'll be spendin' the rest of our lives searchin' for the goddamned place.'

Murdoch subjected the new members of the gang, shifty-eyed, liquor-smelling-breath characters, to an assaying glance. He tagged them as drifters, men who were looking for work that didn't raise any sweat to do it. Men, he opined who would only kill if it meant no risk to themselves. He was banking on his reading of them. He wanted them to back him up when the time came to confront Brown Bear with his grand plan.

A wolf-smiling Casper drew out his rifle. 'Let's show the sonsuvbitches we're here and mean business,' he said.

Right now was the time he told Brown Bear his plan, Murdoch thought. He kneed his mount close alongside Casper's.

'You're goin' off at half-cock again, Casper,' he said. 'Ain't you learned your lesson yet?'

'What the hell do you mean, lesson!' Casper snarled. 'Those bastards in that shack are goin' to pay for killin' my buddies!'

'They weren't buddies of mine and Skeeter's, Casper. Me and him joined this outfit to steal some horses and enjoy what we make on sellin' them, not to fight a goddamned private war. And I reckon those boys from the fort came ridin' with us for the same reason.' Out of the corner of his eye Murdoch saw three unshaven chins nod in agreement. So far so good, he thought. 'You go ahead, Casper, cut loose with the piece and let us all sit here and see who comes shootin' at us from outa those trees. As I told you before, the mounties who saw off your buddies could still be hangin' around.'

Casper's face became red blotched with anger as he looked across at Brown Bear for support for making a fight of it. The 'breed's face was as unreadable as a full-blood's. He would favour going in hollering and shooting to kill, but he could read the signs regarding the men he had hired at the fort as clearly as the big Yankee. If they thought the taking of the horses meant spilling their blood unnecessarily, they would rib-kick it back to Fort Whoop-up. Then the big man and his partner would quit and for the second time he would have lost a gang. Before he could assert his authority over his makeshift gang by stating his views on how the raid should go, which, responding to the majority feeling of his gang, would be a less war-like approach than Casper's, he heard the little Yankee speak.

'You just ponder on what my pard has just told you, Casper,' Skeeter said, realizing he and Murdoch were running along the thin, dangerous line of keeping the rustlers in check, enabling them to get what they came for without any harm coming to the Pevrils. It was time he laid the pressure thick on the 'breed.

'If we do go in as you suggest, Casper,' he continued, 'burnin' and killin', how long do you think you'll be able to celebrate gettin' your revenge for the killin' of your buddies, eh? Christ, man, we'll be double-marked. We're wanted by the law now; the killin' of women, and there must be females in that shack, will raise such a stink in the territory that it will have the Canadian Army crawlin' all over these woods all worked up to shoot dead on sight any character they spot within rifle range. They'll find Fort Whoop-up and kill or hang every mother's son they find skulking there. Me and Murdoch don't fancy facin' all that hassle, Casper, even if our own brothers had been shot. We want the horses the easiest way we can get them.' Skeeter shot him a withering glance before turning away.

'You tell me how we get those horses, easy like, Murdoch,' Brown Bear asked, as a mumbling, cursing Casper rammed his rifle back into its boot.

Murdoch favoured him with a skin-deep grin. 'Well, I won't persuade the rancher myself to part with his horses, that's Skeeter's job.' Skeeter played his part showing a surprised, 'How the hell do I do that?' look. 'Whoever comes out of that shack, a female I hope, Skeeter will sneak up on her and lay his big knife across her tender throat. Then he'll show himself to those in the house, warnin' them if they don't give up their horses he'll cut her throat.' Murdoch's grin became smug. 'I reckon that threat should make them do our biddin' without any fuss. They won't dare to call our bluff.'

Skeeter gave a cruel-eyed glare of a smile as if itching to use his knife, giving the impression to Brown Bear he had Indian blood running through his veins.

The plan got more nods of approval from the Fort Whoop-up men. It suited them just fine. If the owner of the horses rated them higher than the life of one of his kin then the bloodthirsty little Yankee would be the first to find out, he would get himself all shot to hell, warning them it was time to cut and run for it.

Brown Bear saw the significant glances passing between the three of them and again he knew that if he wanted a gang to boss over he would have to fall in with Murdoch's line of thinking. He had to admit it was good tactics to risk the life of only one man. If the little knife man got himself killed then he could do it his way, with guns and fire.

'OK, Murdoch,' he said. 'We'll play it as you say. The rest of us will cover the shack in case things don't work out as you say.'

Murdoch breathed a silent but deep sigh of relief. Now it all depended on the second unknown factor: Pevril's going along with his scheme.

A screwed-up-nerved Pevril peered out of the porch window for the first sightings of the rustlers, worrying himself sick wondering if it was going to be killing trouble or turn out to be of no danger to him and his family as Murdoch had told Pete he would try and make it so.

He had listened, blood icing over, as the constable told him of all that had happened to him since leaving the ranch with his prisoner. And he had cockily thought he and the boys had scared off any would-be horse-thieves for good.

'And you say Murdoch and Skeeter are passin' themselves off as Yankee bad-asses and have joined up with Brown Bear?' he had said.

'That's right, Mr Pevril,' replied Pete. 'They've certainly fooled the 'breed; he believes them to be a couple of killers. The big Yankee, by riding with the new gang Brown Bear's raising, thinks that when they hit you again he can prevent any shooting being done by them. How he intends to do that I don't rightly know. He must have some sort of a plan. Though pulling it off will depend on you, Mr Pevril. You'll have to be willing to hand over your horses without putting up a fight.'

Pete saw the rancher's face colour in barely controlled rage and expected him to order him off his land for daring to suggest such a cowardly action on his part.

'You'll not lose out, Mr Pevril,' he said hurriedly, in an attempt to mollify the old man. 'Murdoch hopes to be able to give you back the horses, or pay you for what they're worth. He wants your stock as a lure to help him to rope in some Yankee rustlers they're hunting. If you don't mind me telling you, Mr Pevril, it's the only option you've got. When Brown Bear and his boys come riding in without my and the two Yankee regulators' fire-power to back you up, this place will go up in flames.' Pete thin-smiled. 'I can't help you, I'm supposed to be dead.'

Pevril gave Pete a hard-eyed look. 'What the hell do you mean *supposed dead?* You're either dead, or you ain't!'

'Well, Casper,' Pete said, 'he's the fella you captured, was all set to shoot me for real, but Murdoch said it made sense to kill me silently being that the other *riflemen with me* on the ridge could still be around. Brown Bear thinks they're mounties. Brown Bear agreed and Skeeter led me into the brush and "killed" me, or so Brown Bear and Casper believe. That's why I've to keep low when they ride back this way. If I'm spotted, Murdoch and Skeeter are dead. Then you and your family will be next, not forgetting yours truly.'

'He sure is a devious thinker, this Murdoch,' Pevril said.

'Both of them must be used to out-thinking the men they're hunting down to have stayed alive so long as regulators,' replied Pete. 'I've one more favour to ask, Mr Pevril,' he continued. 'I'd be obliged if you could supply me with a saddle horse.

Those no-good horse-thieves took mine. Brown Bear don't want my body or my gear found so I couldn't be posted missing till I was overdue reporting in from my patrol. That will give him the time to do what he intends doing here.'

Pevril sat, shoulders bowed, dejected. Pete was right, as much as it galled him. He and his boys had no chance of beating off the raiders a second time. The sons-of-bitches wouldn't risk getting shot again. The flaming torches would be hurtling down from the back ridge. The stark choice facing him was the lives of his family or his horses. Which he knew, was no choice at all. His kin would always come first.

'I'm not overjoyed to do so, Pete,' he said, 'but I'll go along with Murdoch and Skeeter's plan. It's the only chance I'll have of protectin' my home and family.' His body stiffened, face and gaze hardening in resolve when he spoke again. 'Though if our Yankee friends' scheme goes sour then Brown Bear and the border rats who ride with him have one helluva fight on their hands and Murdoch and Skeeter will have to take their chances with the rest of us.' He got to his feet, thin-smiling. 'I'll get you that mount, Pete; it ain't every day I get to see a "dead" man climb up on to a horse. You can also take the four ranch horses with you or that sonuvabitch, Brown Bear will clear me out of mounts.'

He'd had a tough job persuading Harvey and Jim to accept the possible handing over of the horses to the rustlers without a fight. 'It don't exactly go down well with me, boys,' he said, 'but there's your ma and grandma to consider. The next time Brown Bear and his men come, if Mr Murdoch and Mr Skeeter's plan don't work, they'll not ride in bold-assed. We'll be lucky to pull off a shot at them before this place goes up in flames.' He smiled at his grandsons. 'Besides, we ain't actually losing our horses. So when you go about your chores act naturally; I'll tell your ma and grandma to do likewise. We don't want Brown Bear to think we knew of his raid. Mr Murdoch and Mr Skeeter are runnin' with wolves for our sakes.'

Pevril took another look out of the window, almost wishing the rustlers were standing outside, then things would be finally settled, in their favour he fervently prayed.

'Someone's comin' out!' Brown Bear said, giving a death's head grin as the cabin door opened. 'It's a young female, Skeeter, just what you wanted.' His grin froze into a look of surprise, the little Yankee wasn't beside his buddy, and he hadn't seen him go. The sneaky bastard definitely had Indian blood in him.

Murdoch grinned mockingly back at him. 'Skeeter ain't an *hombre* who lets grass grow beneath his feet. You'll get the horses soon, the easy way, you'll see,' he said. Or so he was hoping, or he and Skeeter would be facing one hell of a gunfight.

Miriam Pevril walked across to the barn carrying a basket of grain for the hens. She was trying to act as naturally as she could knowing that the rustlers were about to raid them again. Her father-in-law had confidently told her that everything would work out fine. Mr Murdoch and Mr Skeeter who were with the raiders would see that they came to no harm. Miriam knew he was as worried as she was and only spoke so boldly to keep up her and the boys' spirits. She stepped inside the barn and stopped dead in her tracks, giving out a low frightened gasp. Mr Skeeter was standing in front of her.

Skeeter grinned at her. 'Don't fret none, everything's goin' to be OK, ma'am,' he said. 'I take it you know what's goin' on and the old man is playin' along with us?'

Miriam, nerves still jumping, managed a dry-throated, 'Yes.'

'Good,' replied Skeeter. 'Now, when we go back to the house I'll have a knife at your throat, so you look real scared. We've got to fool some hardcases up on the ridge.' Skeeter's smile reached his ears. 'Now, what about a scream to start off with?'

Pevril grabbed for his rifle at the sound of Miriam's scream and was out on the porch in a couple of strides cradling the Winchester to his chest as he levered a shell into the breech. His moment of truth was here. Was it for real, or part of the two Yankees' plan, he thought, wildly.

Skeeter walked slowly towards the house, holding Miriam in front of him as a living shield with one arm, his other hand fisting the knife. 'You drop that rifle, mister!' he called out. 'And get the rest of them in the shack outside on the porch, unarmed, *pronto*, or this woman gets dead!'

For one fearful moment seeing Skeeter's savage scowling face, the old man thought that he and Pete had been fooled by the two Americans, their so-called plan only a trick to get the rustlers close in without being shot at. Then he saw Skeeter wink at him and almost cried out with relief. He lowered his rifle to the boards and called over his shoulder, 'Harvey, Jim, come on out! Leave your guns inside! The bastards have your mother! You'd better come out as well, Ma!' He waited till the three were lined up behind him, then putting on a scowling mask of a face, as false as Skeeter's, he said, 'We're all here, you sonuvabitch, there's no need to harm the girl!'

'OK, boys! Come on down!' Skeeter yelled. 'We've got ourselves some horses!' He lowered his voice and spoke to the rancher. 'Things shouldn't get out of hand, but if they do me and Murdoch will cover you till you get back indoors, you as well, ma'am. Then start shooting so me and my pard can find a hole to jump into before our short-time buddies plug us.'

Eleven

The operation was going smoothly. The horses were herded out of the corral ready for the drive to Fort Whoop-up. Skeeter's arm was getting tired holding the knife, worrying that if his hand dropped, the razor-edged blade would really draw blood from the woman.

Yet he hadn't to relax his pretended fierceness. While even Murdoch was helping to get the horses out of the corral Casper was still finding time to cast killing looks in his direction. Brown Bear to keep his gang together had agreed there should be no unnecessary killings, Skeeter had doubts about Casper accepting that decision. He was still having bad thoughts against the Pevrils.

At last all the horses were bunched up on

the trail ready to move out and Skeeter saw Brown Bear peel off from the herd and come riding down towards him. He also noticed Murdoch pull clear of the dust haze to where he had a clear view of him and the Pevrils, a move he had expected from Murdoch, having worked together in tricky situations for so long. His partner was in a position where he could back him up if Brown Bear was coming to tell him he had had a change of heart and intended torching the cabin and shooting down the male members of the Pevril family.

Brown Bear drew up his mount in front of Skeeter. He shot a baleful-eyed look at the Pevrils. 'Any trouble from them?' he asked.

'No trouble at all, Brown Bear,' replied Skeeter. 'This purty female saw to that.' He put his knife menacingly closer to Miriam's throat. Miriam, playing her part, gave a sobbing cry of fear, that brought a cruel grin to the 'breed's face.

'We're ready to move out,' Brown Bear said. 'When we've made an hour or so on the trail I'll send Casper back to pick you up.' The cold, skin-deep smile returned. 'Otherwise you could get yourself lost in all that timber.' He gave the Pevrils another hard-eyed glare before pulling his horse round and riding back to the herd. Skeeter watched him go with a feeling of great relief. They had been lucky to have persuaded the three Fort Whoop-up men to fall in with their plan to take the horses without shedding blood. That had put pressure on the 'breed to OK it for, like Casper, he wanted to get blood for blood from the Pevrils.

The thought of getting even with the Pevrils was passing through Brown Bear's mind. Once the cattle he would get in exchange for the horses had been sold, one dark night he would Indian-up on the ranch and have the belated, pleasurable revenge of burning it to the ground.

Pete, well back from the ranch, though a keen watcher of all that had been happening there, lowered his rifle on seeing Brown

Bear give the orders to move out the horses. Murdoch's wild-ass plan had worked, no harm had come to the Pevrils. He hoped Murdoch's and Skeeter's second part of their plan would go just as favourably for them. Skeeter had told him to keep low, but if Brown Bear had decided to come in shooting there would have been no reason to keep his presence a secret.

Murdoch and Skeeter would have had to break their cover to stop the 'breed from massacring the Pevrils and would need all the fire-power they could get to back them up in a gunfight close up to a bunch of killers.

Once the fast-driven horses had dropped behind the first ridge, Skeeter released his hold on Miriam and slid the knife into its sheath. Grinning, he said, 'We can all breathe easy again, folks. Get on with your chores but keep close to the house; Casper is comin' back for me and he'll expect to see me still threatenin' you all.'

'I ain't sweated as much since I first met

Johnny Reb at Shiloh,' Doug Pevril said. 'How the hell you and the big fella stick it out doin' what you do has me beat.'

'I wonder that myself sometimes,' replied Skeeter. 'I used to think it was better than tendin' sheep, now I ain't so sure. Though I must admit this job's goin' all me and Murdoch's way, so far that is. We've got the Canadian boys practically in the bag, which we ain't bein' paid to rope in. The horses should help us to round-up the Montana cattle-lifters we're after. Then all we've got to do is burn down that thieves' hide-out, Fort Whoop-up, to round off Constable Slade's happy time.'

The old rancher grinned. 'It sure must be hell for you and Mr Murdoch when you're real busy I reckon. Now I'd better get some chores done before that asshole rides back in.'

Skeeter sat on the porch cleaning his nails with his knife but also keeping a watchful eye for signs of Casper riding down from the high ground. Looking at his pocket-watch he judged it was time to put on his act again. 'OK, folks!' he called out. 'Get yourselves back to cowerin' on the porch, Casper should be showin' his ugly mug soon!'

Casper didn't ride right up to the cabin, he closed in on foot, rifle in hand, all set to plug the weasel-faced son-of-a-bitch who had fooled him and Brown Bear.

Riding down from the high ridges by a side trail he had seen Skeeter sitting on the porch on his own. This had puzzled him at first. Had the little Yank slaughtered all the Pevrils? He had heard no sounds of gunfire. Then he saw the female, the one whose throat Skeeter was willing to slit, followed by the rest of the family, step out on to the porch, smiling real friendly like at Skeeter.

It wasn't clear to him who Skeeter and his big buddy were, lawmen, bounty hunters, whoever; it didn't matter, they were definitely not the rustlers they said they were. Killing the sneaky bastards was all that mattered, starting with the knife man, Mr Skeeter.

Casper drew up his mount with a vicious neck-yanking tug. Pulling out his rifle he swung down from his saddle with black hatred eating at his heart. He took a long look about him, sensing that the mountie Skeeter was supposedly to knife, would be alive and close by. He would accept that risk to get in real close to Skeeter so he could have the pleasure of seeing his face when the bastard saw that he had been outsmarted. Then he would gut-shoot him, his dying screams loud enough to be heard by Dutch in Hell. Casper hoped Skeeter would live long enough to see the Pevrils and their home going up in flames.

For once in his professional life as a manhunter, Skeeter's highly-tuned sense of self-preservation let him down. He didn't know he was in deep trouble until he heard Casper's voice telling him to sit tight or the woman would get the first shell.

'And unlike your friend here, lady,' Casper

continued, 'I mean it.' The Pevril family froze in horrified silence on the porch.

Skeeter gimlet-eyed Casper as he slowly inched his hands away from his body, palms resting on the boards, right hand tilted slightly hiding the knife lying at his side. He would save his cursing for being caught by the balls until he had killed Casper.

The rustler had made one big mistake: he had the edge and should have kept it by shooting him out of hand. The foolish son-of-a-bitch felt the need to gloat over the fact he had the drop on him. Skeeter was a great believer in the maxim that if it's your intention to kill a man then don't threaten to do it, pull off a shot or two and have done with it. As long as Casper was basking in his moment of glory he had a chance, a way-out one, of pulling himself out of this hairy situation. Skeeter gave a silent grunt of satisfaction as his fingers slid over the handle of the knife. The odds against him were beginning to lower.

Pete saw his former prisoner creeping up

to the house, hidden from Skeeter's view. He cursed loudly, the Yankees' plan was coming apart. Casper was too far away for him to fire with the certainty of a kill. A winged Casper would be a danger, shooting down Skeeter and some of the Pevrils before they could take cover. He got to his feet, it was time he did some pussyfooting of his own.

Casper, savouring his hold on Skeeter to the full, noticed a look come on to the woman's face that shouldn't be there. Not when he was fierce-eying her and had a rifle pointed at her. She was seeing something that boded ill for him. Face twisted in angry alarm he spun round.

He saw definite proof that the mountie wasn't dead, the son-of-a-bitch was trying to sneak up on him. Dirty-mouthing, he triggered off a shot from the hip at him. Pete, surprised by the speed of Casper's action, felt a sickening, hammer-like blow in his right arm, the pain causing him to drop his rifle, and do his own bout of cursing. He waited, all hunched up, for Casper's second shot, the killing shot.

Skeeter got the break he didn't expect. In one sweeping movement the knife was in his hand and in an underarm throw, was winging on its deadly way to its target.

Casper's smile of triumph stiffened into a grimace of infinite pain as the flashing blade plunged deep into his neck. He buckled slowly at the knees as the blood poured thick from his throat to fall face down on to the ground, still holding his rifle in a clawed-fingered grip of a rapidly dying man. With drawn and cocked pistol, Skeeter ran across to where Casper lay. Though he looked as good as dead it didn't do to act careless twice.

Doug Pevril and the two boys sped over to a pain-racked-faced Pete clutching at his right arm, Pete opining that it was only his mountie pride keeping him on his feet. He didn't want to hit the dirt in front of two kids.

Skeeter, on checking that Casper was on

his way to Hell walked across to them as the two boys were helping Pete to make it to the house. 'You could've got yourself killed, Pete,' he said. 'But I'm sure glad you showed up when you did. Casper was worked up into a real killin' mood. Though he wasn't expectin' to do the dying.'

'I feel as though I'm headin' that way now, Skeeter,' replied Pete. He forced out a weak, painful grin. 'The mounties always get their man, or so I was told when I joined the Force, but this time the man got me if you hadn't been so slick with that knife of yours.'

'You gave me the chance to use it, friend,' Skeeter said. 'Now I've to come up with an explanation of what happened here that will not have the 'breed thinkin' suspicious thoughts about me and Murdoch. And it'll have to be quick before the horses get too far along the owlhoot trail to Fort Whoop-up bein' the dead and departed Casper was to be my guide.' He grinned. 'Don't worry, I'll come up with something, Pete. You go on inside and let the good ladies fix up your arm.'

Skeeter did some rapid thinking as he gave Doug Pevril a helping hand to sling Casper's body over his horse so the old rancher could take it up on the ridge above the house for burial. Pevril saw him smile.

'Another wild one, Skeeter?' he said.

'What else?' replied Skeeter. 'Me and Murdoch are wild boys runnin' with wild boys. Though this "plan" of mine will need your boys' help.'

'You just ask them for it, Skeeter. You'll get it, never fear,' the rancher said. 'Now I'll go and see Casper decently planted.' He smiled. 'I've got a regular growin' Boot Hill up on that ridge.'

Murdoch kept casting apprehensive glances over his shoulder. By his reckoning Skeeter should have been riding in with Casper by now. He hoped the little runt's luck hadn't run out. If it had his could be heading for a dive very soon. He looked around, taking in the men he would have to kill if their cover was blown, and he wanted to stay alive. The 'breed would have to be first, then Casper, if things were turning out for the worst. What the hell, he thought, life was full of disappointments.

Brown Bear was having his own worries, like two men short on the drive. The lateness of Casper and the little Yankee showing up could mean they had been shot, or captured by the rest of the mountie patrol they had clashed with at the ranch. It would be an hour or so at the speed they were pushing the horses before they reached the well-hidden cut-off trail to Fort Whoop-up.

A gunfight up on horses with sharp-shooting riflemen was the last thing he wanted. The three Fort Whoop-up bums would quit on him as soon as the hot lead began to fly. Then it would be the second bunch of horses he had lost, his dealings with Clanton over before they had got going. If trouble was coming along their back trail he wanted someone he could trust to hold it at bay a piece, and win them some time to allow them to get the horses off the main trail.

He eased his horse back till Murdoch, bringing up the drag, came alongside him. 'Hang back with me, Murdoch,' he said. 'Casper's late. Him and your buddy could have run into trouble and that trouble could be headin' this way. This is as good a spot as any to face it.' Then, raising his voice, he yelled, 'Keep 'em movin'! You know where the turn off is! We'll catch you up!'

Murdoch followed Brown Bear back along the trail till they were clear of the timber and could see the trail snaking its way across the open ground below them. The 'breed guided his horse into the brush on his side of the trail and dismounted, holding his rifle. Murdoch did likewise on his side of the trail.

Murdoch was thinking if things turned out as bad as he was opining, that Casper had somehow put paid to Skeeter, he would have no trouble at all in avenging his partner's death. Casper and the 'breed would only live as long as it took him to put the Winchester to his shoulder and trigger off two shots. Then he would catch up with the horses and put the fear of God in the Fort Whoop-up boys by riding down on them with pistols cutting loose in both hands. He realized it would need another mad-assed plan to tackle the Montana rustlers, if they were at the fort, but he had more pressing things on his mind right now to start thinking of one, such as contemplating the killing time.

Brown Bear saw the smoke clouds billowing above the lower ridges. He cold-smiled across at him. 'It looks as though Casper's been busy,' he said. 'That's the ranch goin' up in flames.'

Murdoch didn't answer him. His worst fears looked as though they had been justified. If Casper had torched the ranch he must have got the better of Skeeter, his partner would have put his life on the line to keep the Pevrils from coming to any harm.

He would have to accept Skeeter was dead. Stone-faced he picked up his rifle. When Casper showed up he would blow him and the 'breed out of their saddles.

Skeeter, riding hard, twisted ass in his saddle to eye the growing column of smoke. He gave a grunt of satisfaction. It definitely looked as though the Pevril ranch was burning. He hoped he hadn't started the fire too late for Brown Bear to see the smoke and come to the same conclusion, or the Pevril boys would have sweated, dragging the brushwood to start the fire, for nothing. The 'burning down' of the ranch was to back up his story of how Casper must have met his end.

'Rider comin' in!' Brown Bear called out. 'It looks like your buddy, Murdoch! Where the hell's Casper?' he added, puzzle-faced.

Murdoch's face almost split into one of his beaming smiles as Skeeter drew up beside him in a dust-raising halt. He knew whatever was burning down there it couldn't be the Pevril place, not when

Skeeter was sitting on his horse in front of him. It looked as though there had been trouble and Casper had lost out.

'Casper didn't show up, Brown Bear!' Skeeter burst out. 'I couldn't wait any longer for him in case I lost your trail!' He grinned wolfishly at the 'breed. 'I put a torch to the cabin just to keep the bastards occupied somewhat savin' their bits and pieces while I lit out.'

'You've been lucky, Skeeter,' Murdoch said. 'I reckon Casper must have had a run in with those other mounties you spoke of, Brown Bear.' He was nudging the 'breed into the way Skeeter wanted him to reason.

Murdoch could see the 'breed's face working as he chewed over this latest piece of bad news. He saw him give Skeeter a penetrating look as if trying to read his mind, being a natural-born suspicious man doubting what he had heard. He was wasting his time, Murdoch knew, Skeeter was the smoothest forked-tongued *hombre* on either side of the border. He could fool

St Peter if he ever made it to the Pearly Gates.

'It looks that way, Murdoch,' Brown Bear said, almost snarling the words out. 'It ain't any good stayin' here yappin' about it. Let's get back to the herd in case those two redcoat sonsuvbitches start to track us. If Casper can manage it he'll catch up with us.' He dug his spurs savagely into his horse's flanks that sent it galloping back along the trail.

'Will Casper catch up with us, Skeeter?' Murdoch asked.

Skeeter grinned. 'Not unless he's sprouted angel's wings, Murdoch, if he's made it to Heaven and not Hell where he belongs.'

Murdoch smiled back at him. 'The show's still on the road then. Mr Ritchie would be pleased if he knew.'

Twelve

They had been two days at Fort Whoop-up and Murdoch, sitting on his own in the camp's store-cum-bar, felt highly satisfied with the way things were running for him and Skeeter, who was with one of the new men guarding the horses in a draw a couple of miles away. In his professional opinion the case was almost wrapped up. While they hadn't actually got the stealers of Ritchie's cattle in custody, or shot dead, it would be only a matter of time before they could report back to the rancher telling him his cattle-lifting troubles were over. Murdoch gave a relaxed smile. No more sweating off pounds, he thought, thinking up crack-brained plans.

Earlier in the day, he had seen a man ride into the fort and have words with Brown

Bear that brought a smile to the 'breed's hatchet-hewn face, and his. The bringer of Brown Bear's favourable news was the man whom Skeeter had tried to scalp. A Slash Y man. The last piece of the case had fallen into place, Surtees's crew were the rustlers and must be heading for the fort with another bunch of stolen beef.

After the horses and cattle had been exchanged, Brown Bear would suddenly lose two of his gang; he and Skeeter would be dogging the Slash Y men trailing the horses back to Montana. Murdoch opined, what with holding false Canadian bills of ownership for the horses they would be corralled at the Slash Y, as legally bought stock.

Their next move would be to ride out to Surtees's spread and accuse Surtees, face-to-face, of being involved in the rustling here and in Canada. Their words as Cattlemen's Association agents would be proof enough to make the charge stick in front of a cattlemen's judge. Further evidence, if wanted, could come from old man Pevril who would be able to identify his stock and the manner of their taking.

Naturally, not wanting to be a pair of would-be Daniels, they would enter the lion's den of the Slash Y backed up by a well-armed posse of Ritchie's men just in case the hard men who rode for Surtees, facing a hanging, decided to make a fight of it.

Before he and Skeeter left the fort, Murdoch thought, the 'breed would have to be taken care of. He couldn't be left to seek his revenge against the Pevrils. They were beholden to the old man to prevent that happening. As for the equally honour-bound promise to Pete, the destruction of Fort Whoop-up, Murdoch reckoned he could safely leave that task to Skeeter. He was the dynamite expert. He would have a word with him about the timing of the spectacular event when he ended his watch over the horses.

Murdoch ceased his ruminating as he

heard the sound of voices outside the shack. The 'breed walked in first. Followed by the mean-faced boss man he had seen in the saloon in Red Butte talking to the two men who had been dogging him and Skeeter. He saw the rustler's eyes flickering in surprised puzzlement. He gave him a non-committal grin back. After all, Murdoch thought, we're kind of partners, till I see you strung up.

A faint warning bell was sounding in Clanton's ears. For a panhandler drifter the big man certainly got around. In Red Butte he had accepted him and his partner as they seemed; here in Fort Whoop-up territory, where there weren't any gold-bearing streams, he wasn't so sure. Something about him didn't ring true.

Lassiter, coming in behind Clanton, was also surprised. He was gazing at a man he thought was four states south of here. Reacting fast, he pushed past Clanton, cursing and yanking out his pistol. Murdoch's recognition of Lassiter was slower. He was halfway out of his seat, pistol part clear of its holster when Lassiter's savage swinging gun struck him a sickening blow on the head and drove him back down into his seat to slump across the table, out to the wide.

'What the hell's goin' on!' Brown Bear cried. 'That's Murdoch, one of my boys!'

Lassiter gave him a sneering look as he slid his pistol back into its sheath. 'He may be one of your boys,' he said, 'but his heart and soul ain't in it. Unless he's given up bein' a regulator. Usually he's in harness with a foxy-faced weed of a man, goes by the name of Skeeter.' Lassiter stopped speaking when he saw the expression on Brown Bear's face. 'He's one of your boys as well, ain't he?' He turned fiercely on Clanton. 'What sort of operation are the pair of you runnin' here, hirin' no-good regulators. The bastards must have known every move you made. It's a miracle you ain't been strung up already! Where's Skeeter now?'

It took several moments for Brown Bear to find his voice. He was attempting to come to terms with the full extent of how his 'boys' had fooled him. He knew now the pair had been in on the killing of his men at the ranch, there had been no mountie patrol, just one redcoat. And Skeeter hadn't knifed him. Casper, he accepted, was dead, killed by the mountie or Skeeter. His gut feeling told him it was Skeeter's doing. The two sons-of-bitches had made him lose face in front of his Yankee partners. Only their long, painful, deaths would wipe out that insult.

Face all bone, his Indian blood running wild, he said, 'He's guardin' the horses.' He bared his teeth in a fierce grin. 'You'll hear his screams all the way back here as he finds out how long a Sioux can inflict pain on a man before he finally dies.'

'Hold on, Brown Bear,' Clanton said. 'We want Skeeter alive, leastways till we persuade him and his pard to tell us what their next moves were goin' to be. For all we know there could be a mountie's posse nearby waitin' to move in on us at a signal from them.' Clanton's smile was as savage as the 'breed's. 'You can tell him that if he don't come in peaceful like you'll start carvin' up his pard.'

Lassiter laughed derisively. 'That threat won't work, Clanton,' he said. 'I know those bastards, they almost roped me in once. Whatever else you may think of them, they're professionals. They won't quit an assignment even if both their mas were bein' held by the parties they were bein' paid to bring in. Send Slats and Bub, Clanton. Skeeter will naturally take them as his relief when they go riding in. Then, when they get the chance, throw down on the sonuvabitch.'

'That makes sense, Brown Bear,' Clanton said. 'I'll see to it. And we'd better warn the rest of the boys to be on the alert just in case we have to move out fast. You stay here, Lassiter, and keep an eye on the big fella, tie him to the chair. When he comes to you can talk to him about the old times and how Brown Bear intends to work on him and his pard with his knife. I'll send Phil along to keep you company.' He turned to Brown Bear. 'Let's go and tell Slats and Bub what's expected of them,' he said. 'All this wonderin' what could be buildin' up against us has me worried.'

'Looks like our relief comin' in, Skeeter,' the Fort Whoop-up man said, on seeing two riders rapidly approaching the camp. 'I ain't seen those fellas before,' he added, as the riders came nearer. 'I guess they must be two of the Montana boys who've brought in a bunch of Yankee cows.'

Skeeter hadn't to guess who they were. The rider on the left was the man he had thrown a scare into with his knife. The other rider had been with him on the street, checking on him and Murdoch. Now he knew for certain the Slash Y crew were the rustlers plaguing the territory and Surtees must be their paymaster. Skeeter reckoned, like Murdoch had, their job was about all wrapped up.

The thought of why Brown Bear hadn't

sent the other two Fort Whoop-up men to relieve them passed briefly through his mind, then he opined the Montana men would want to check on the horses they were going to drive back over the border. Though that didn't stop him from gimlet-eying the riders. Every man he and Murdoch met in their dangerous trade had to be looked on as hostile till events proved the opposite. That precaution had kept them alive.

'Swing round to his left, Bub, when we stroll in,' Slats said, softly as they drew up their horses. 'Then we've got the regulatin' sonuvabitch between us. Clanton wants him alive, but that don't mean we can't plug him real bad if he makes a fight of it. We're two of Clanton's boys comin' across to relieve you,' he called out. Then, all smiles as he dismounted, he said, 'That coffee sure smells good.'

Skeeter knew all about forked-tongued smiles, Murdoch was a past master in wearing them, and he was gazing at one such smile right now. And that puzzled him. Why would a man he had made to eat crow try to fool him into thinking he was all friendly. The bastard must still be sore at him and there he was grinning at him as though he was greeting a long-lost brother. He flashed the pair a grin just as bogus and said, 'Come on in, boys, and help yourselves to a mug, it's just been made.'

Then Skeeter noticed the two men edge apart as they came closer, and he was no longer puzzled. He was looking at trouble. Somehow his and Murdoch's cover had been blown. He couldn't spend time wondering what had happened to his partner, he was concentrating on the Slash Y men's hands.

Men, he knew, would try and fool you by their looks and sweet-talking, like the oily-smiling bastard coming towards him, but what they did with their hands was the dead give away. No amount of smiling could cover the moving of hands sneaking towards pistols. When he saw fingers straying downwards the wide-smiling rustler was dead. He was the more dangerous of the two, he had a personal reason to cut loose at him.

His buddy, so he could be able to tell what the situation was back at the fort, and Murdoch's fate, he would only wing. He would also have to take in the likelihood of the Fort Whoop-up man backing up the Slash Y men's play. So he could be facing three guns. Still squatting at the fire, showing no signs of concern, Skeeter leaned forward slightly, allowing his pistol to slip part way out of its holster, the few inches that could determine whether he lived or died.

Slats's impatience to show Skeeter he was the man who would be calling the tune from now on in made him give up his softly-softly approach. It was an eagerness that cost him his life. With his face a snarling mask of triumph he clawed wildly for his gun. His hasty, ill-aimed shot kicked up the embers of the fire in front of Skeeter's face.

Skeeter's pistol seemed to jump into his hand and with a split-second aim, still crouching low, he triggered off three rapidly fired loads.

Two shells raised red-tinged dust spurts on the front of Slats's vest before he could fire again, dropping him to the ground as rigid as a felled cottonwood, his grimace fixed for all eternity. Bub made a lot more fuss when the third shell shattered the elbow of his gun arm into bloody pieces of bone and flesh. He howled like a kicked cur dog, doubling up with pain, his pistol thudding to the ground, unfired.

Skeeter was up on his feet, pistol swinging on to the Fort Whoop-up man, eyes glinting madly. 'Make your play, pilgrim,' he grated. 'I'm in a real killin' mood!'

His former horse-lifting partner gazed back at him, white-faced, slack-jawed at the sudden turn of events. He had no idea of the nature of the dispute the three must have had for it to come to a head in a shoot-out and he wasn't about to take sides. Definitely not on the Montana boys' side. Suddenly going into the horse-lifting business was looking like a bad move on his part. 'Mister,' he mouthed, hoarsely, 'I ain't no pistol man, I ain't even a regular horse-thief. And I sure had no part in the Montana boys' plan to gun you down.' Slowly he began to unbuckle his gunbelt.

'Good move,' said Skeeter, as the gunbelt dropped at the rustler's feet. 'Now just stand there at peace with yourself and you'll be OK while I have a talk to the fella I winged.'

Bub's animal howls had dropped to a low-pitched keening sound. 'You've busted my arm for good!' he sobbed, as Skeeter came up to him. 'You no-good sonuvabitch!'

'That I have, pilgrim,' replied Skeeter. 'And I'll bust your other arm if you don't tell me how my pard is farin' and how you found out we're regulators.'

'It was Monte Lassiter, he's just joined the gang who knew who your pard really was,' Bub gasped, painfully. 'And he's OK,

Clanton's got him under guard in the store.'

Well I'll be damned, Skeeter thought, Lassiter. That wild boy is a long way from his stomping ground. So was he and Murdoch for that matter. Twice in the past few days it had been proved it was a small world. He would have to make sure this time that the piece of the world Lassiter was gazing at now was the last bit he was ever to see.

'Clanton,' he said. 'Was he the mean-faced *hombre* with you in the saloon at Red Butte?'

'Yeah, that's him,' replied a pain-teared-eyed Bub. 'He's our boss.'

'And him and the 'breed are waitin' for you and that fella lyin' dead on the ground there to bring me back all roped up,' Skeeter said.

'That's what was reckoned,' Bub said. 'Then the 'breed was goin' to work on you and the big fella to find out if you had any backin' keepin' low hereabouts.'

Skeeter's smile was for real this time, Murdoch was alive. The bringing to justice of the rustlers had only been delayed somewhat. The sound of the first stick of dynamite exploding about their ears would be a loud and clear message that they were being hunted down again. Though his first priority had to be the freeing of his partner; Murdoch wouldn't want to miss out on all the excitement.

He fish-eyed Bub. 'Bein' I'm in a charitable mood,' he said. 'I ain't about to hang you, though Mr Ritchie of Montana, who's hirin' me and Murdoch to rid him of vermin like you and the fellas you once rode with, would be most displeased at me not dispatchin' you to Hell where you rightly belong.' Skeeter beckoned for the Fort Whoop-up man to come over and told him he wasn't stringing him up either for being a rustler. 'But I've got more serious business on my mind than haulin' you both to the nearest mountie post so you're free to go. Take care of this fella though till you come to some settlement where he can have his wound seen to. And keep prayin' you don't meet up with a mountie patrol. If they guess you're a coupla rustlers, then you could end up dancin' under a tree after all.'

After the two men had ridden out Skeeter didn't waste any more time burying Slats. He hadn't any to waste on a dead man. Brown Bear and Clanton would be waiting for him coming in as a prisoner, any delay they would guess that something had gone wrong and Murdoch would be as good as dead. Stone-faced, dynamite sticks short-fused, in his pockets, Skeeter headed back to the fort. All set up to start his one-man war.

Thirteen

When Murdoch came to he found himself sitting in a chair with his hands roped to the back of the chair. His head ached as if it had been kicked by a mule and he felt the sticky tightness of dried blood on his right temple and cheek. At a table close by, Lassiter and a Slash Y man he had never seen before, were sitting playing cards. A pistol lay on the table in front of Lassiter. Murdoch kept his chin resting on his chest as though still unconscious and began to assess his chances of escape.

It was no good making a mad-assed attempt, he reasoned. They had neglected to tie his legs to the chair so it would be no problem for him to stand up and kick the table over, send the gun flying, and while his two guards were struggling to get the table off them, make a dash for the door. Then all he had to bank on was that Brown Bear, Clanton, or any of the other rustlers weren't hanging about outside, and he could get up on to his horse with his ass tied to a chair. Which, he thought, was as mad a plan as he had ever come up with.

His best bet was to wait for Skeeter to make his play. Brown Bear would have sent men to bring Skeeter back to the fort on the end of a rope, a task no penny-ante rustler was capable of doing. Skeeter smelt trouble further than any other man could see it coming, and deal with it to his advantage. Through lowered-lidded eyes he watched the card players, all set to act when he heard the sound of Skeeter's calling card. Then by hell, he promised himself, he would kick the son-of-a-bitch Lassiter, clear through the wall of the shack.

Skeeter dismounted well clear of the encampment, walking the rest of the way in, as tensed up as a dog in heat smelling a bitch. Several women were heading towards the stream carrying bundles of washing, which suited Skeeter fine. When the walls came tumbling down, as the Good Book put it, he didn't want any of the camp women getting hurt. Outside one tent he saw three men sitting drinking in the shade. Cataloguing them as Slash Y men, he gave them a wide berth. On seeing no signs of Brown Bear or Clanton he thin-smiled. He would be seeing them soon.

He stopped to light up the straggle-ended cheroot dangling from the corner of his mouth. Then, with a pistol in one hand, a stick of dynamite in the other, he set off to achieve his first objective, the freeing of his partner.

'You're on a good thing, joinin' up with us, Monte,' Murdoch heard the Slash Y man say. 'Once we've seen to the big fella here and his pardner everything will run smoothly again. Purvis who bossed the Canadians before the 'breed took over, didn't kinda fit in with Mr Surtees's thinkin' the way his rustlin' business should be run.' Then he heard how some of the Slash Y crew had ambushed Purvis on his way to the fort with a string of horses and the shooting of Purvis by Clanton. 'We fooled them into thinkin' they had been jumped by a mountie patrol. Now the stupid part-Injun is workin' for half the price Purvis was claimin', Clanton and us pocketing some of the difference.'

Murdoch didn't have to guess what the

'breed's reaction would be if he ever heard he had been duped. He would go rampaging on the warpath against Clanton and his crew. His thoughts of how he could pass on to the 'breed what he had heard without Clanton silencing him for good before he could speak was suddenly, and noisily cut short by an explosion that blew in the 'dobe built end wall of the shack. Windows shattered, roof beams and roofing came crashing down, narrowly missing Murdoch.

Lassiter and Phil, nearest to the dynamite blast, hurled to the floor, part covered by the fallen debris. Lassiter, coughing and spluttering struggled dazedly to his feet. Phil's luck had run out on him. Several long shards of glass had pierced his body with the killing force of flying arrows and he lay unmoving on the floor.

Murdoch, half-blinded by the clouds of dust whirling around, was on his feet. Skeeter sure had style, he thought; a mite dangerous, but the little hellion had given him the break he had been praying for.

Roaring like an angry bear, avoiding upturned chairs and tables, he charged Lassiter. Lassiter gazed round wildly for the pistol that had been on the table, and couldn't see it. He quickly decided he was no match in a hand-to-hand fight with the big bastard bearing down on him, even if he did have his hands tied to the chair. It was definitely cut-and-run time.

Covering his face with his hands, Lassiter half-climbed, half-dived through the nearest window in his mad dash to escape, not feeling the already broken glass slashing blood streaks across his hands and arms. Murdoch swore. The son-of-a-bitch had slipped by him again. Then he heard Skeeter say, 'Are you OK, Murdoch?' He shook his head to clear his vision and saw Skeeter silhouetted in the gaping hole in the wall. 'Yeah, I'm OK,' he replied. 'Considerin' I was almost blown through the front wall.'

'Yeah, well, I'm sorry about that, Murdoch,' Skeeter said. 'I thought the wall was thicker than it was so I used two sticks.'

He looked down at the timber and 'dobe half-covered body. 'But it put paid to your guard.' He picked his way gingerly over the rubble to get to Murdoch.

'I've heard Lassiter is in town,' he said, as he cut the ropes binding Murdoch's hands to the chair, and handed him a pistol.

'You've just missed the bastard,' Murdoch said. 'He was the other guard. He hauled his ass outa that side window when I was about to kick the livin' daylights out of him.'

Skeeter grinned. 'We won't have to miss him a third time or Big Meg will never make us another meal. Now it's time, I reckon, to show those fellas outside who're cuttin' loose at us we ain't a coupla pushovers. We start by gettin' out into the open which, I'll admit, is goin' to be tricky.' Skeeter tapped his coat pockets, bulging with sticks of dynamite. 'But these terrible beauties could help us out somewhat.'

Skeeter walked to the front door and risked a hurried look out, and just as fast drew his head back as a fusillade of shots ripped splinters off the door post. 'Three, or four guns out there, Murdoch,' he said.

'And I reckon there'll be as many out back if we poke our noses through that hole you made,' Murdoch said. 'Not forgettin' Monte Lassiter at the side, prayin' to get a shot at us.'

Skeeter didn't answer him, he was touching a blasting stick fuse with his cheroot. He reached out through the door to awkwardly throw the dynamite to his left. The bang came almost immediately. Skeeter grinned. 'That's one gun less.'

Clanton ate dirt, fast, as chunks of earth and stones rained down on him. In the centre of the searing red flash of the explosion he saw one of his crew's body hurtling backwards, arms outstretched as if grabbing for air to try and keep his balance. The explosion had brought him and Brown Bear and most of their men rushing out of the women's huts, hastily buttoning up their pants. He was just in time to see Lassiter scrambling through the broken window of the half-demolished store, and the flames of huts behind the store on fire.

It didn't need anyone to tell him that things weren't working out as he had planned them. Slats, Bub, and it looked like Phil as well, could be dead. And now the two bastards were blowing up the rest of his boys in front of his eyes. He raised his head and shouted at Brown Bear, flattened to the ground, several yards away. 'Get your boys round at the back! Those sonsuvbitches ain't comin' outa there anything but dead!' Then, mad-eyed with frustrated anger, he screamed, 'You're dead, you regulatin' scum! We've got you ringed in! You ain't goin' any place but a hole in the ground!'

And that had to be quick. The flames and smoke of the burning huts would be seen clear across the whole of Montana. A half-blind mountie would have no trouble tracking his way here. The easy money rustling operation he had going was finished. Fort Whoop-up's days as a hideout were over.

'Could be he's right, Murdoch,' Skeeter said. 'They're hunkered down too far away for me to use my callin' cards.' He turned from looking out of the doorway to see a smile creeping across his big partner's face. 'You've come up with a plan, ain't you?' he said.

'The best ever,' replied Murdoch, smug-faced. 'That's if our former boss has some proud Sioux blood in him. You stay here, Skeeter, in case they get bold enough to come at us with a rush, I'll go and try grab the 'breed's attention. I think I saw him headin' towards the hole you've put in the back wall.'

Murdoch stood well to one side of the gaping hole and yelled, 'Can you hear me, Brown Bear?' He had to quickly press his body close to the wall as Brown Bear's reply in the shape of a barrage of Winchester shells splashed his face with chipped-off pieces of 'dobe.

The firing eased off for a moment or two and Murdoch heard Brown Bear call back,

'I'll hear you real well when I work on you with my knife.'

Murdoch tried again; making the 'breed see just how big a sucker he had been was his and Skeeter's only chance to get out of the big mess they were in. 'How much is Clanton payin' you, Brown Bear?' he shouted. 'I bet it ain't the fifty-fifty cut Purvis was rakin' in. Clanton was told by his boss to shoot him because he was claimin' too much of the pot. And you were dumb enough to think it was the mounties who ambushed you all. Your Montana so-called pards played you for a dim-witted 'breed, Brown Bear!'

Murdoch held his breath and waited, saying a silent prayer, hoping he had touched the 'breed on a raw, proud nerve, make him mad enough to kill for him and Skeeter.

Brown Bear's face grew meaner; his eyes narrowed with hate. He had suspected that Clanton had got the better of the deal, but not the way he had gone about it. The

Montana men must have been laughing behind his back at his dumbness. He could feel the insult to his pride as physically as the lashes of a bull whip. The anger within him was the ice-cold rage of a full-blood Sioux setting out on a vengeance raid. It would burst into flame when he lifted the scalp on a painfully dying Clanton.

'You stay here!' he snapped to his two men. 'Kill them if they show their faces!' Then he began belly-crawling his way round to the front of the hut, and Clanton.

The Fort Whoop-up men looked at each other, thinking the same thoughts, that it was time to walk away from the rustling business while they could still move around. As if there wasn't enough trouble going on around them in taking on the crazy Yanks and their blasting sticks, another crazy was about to land them in a blood feud with some Montana hardcases. Just as sneaky as Brown Bear, they made their way to the horse lines now, a hive of panicky activity. Wanted by the law, men were hurriedly throwing saddles on their horses, or loading wagons with their belongings and their women, to escape what they thought was the Canadian Army shelling the fort.

Lassiter had flopped down in a shallow hollow, resting awhile, till he came fully to his senses before moving on to take shelter behind a pile of crates. From there he began pulling off rapid shots with his pistol at the shack with hands that were dripping blood. He knew it was a waste of shells, a hitting-out-blindly reaction, but he'd had one hell of a fright, and could have ended up as dead as Phil. And a man who has been pushed to the brink of his grave is entitled to act somewhat wild.

He had thoughts of quitting the gang, getting on to his horse and riding south, as far as the Nations, or Texas, well away from those two hell-raisers in the shack; if he had the money Clanton owed him. There again, thinking more coolly, staying with the gang, and the protection of their guns, were the best odds he would get in seeing that

Murdoch and Skeeter stayed in Canada, dead.

Clanton did some urgent adding up. Counting the 'breed and his two men, his own boys, Stu and Bob, and Lassiter, still in action at the other side of the shack, there was enough of them to rush the hut. Enough guns blazing as they moved in to keep the two bastards away from the windows and the doors so they couldn't use the sticks of dynamite. And the attack had to be right now, to end the stand-off or they would be the ones boxed in by Canadian lawmen.

'Stu!' he called out. 'Go and tell Brown Bear I intend to go fire-ballin' in. When he hears me holler, him and his boys go in with us. Then swing right round the shack and let Lassiter know how we're goin' to play it.'

Stu pulled well back from the action then turned to make his way to the end of the shack, and met Brown Bear face to face. Before he could pass on Clanton's message, Brown Bear swung his knife high across his body slicing through Stu's throat. Stu staggered back several paces, blood pouring from the fearsome gash in his throat. The surprised 'why' look was still showing in his eyes as he folded at the knees and collapsed to the ground.

A grimly smiling Brown Bear listened to Stu's last bubbling, dying breath. It was the first time he had killed with his knife; his Sioux father would have been proud of him. He felt like howling the Sioux death hulloo. Maybe, Brown Bear thought, warily, Clanton had heard Murdoch telling him of his double-dealing and he had sent Stu to kill him. His fingers gripped his knife tighter; his lips drew back in a fierce, defiant snarl. Clanton would soon find out just who was doing the killing.

Yet though he still had the edge of surprise it didn't do to act foolhardily. Clanton wasn't a man easily taken unawares, and there was another Slash Y man with him. As sure-footed silent as a Sioux, Brown Bear, his knife held in front of him, sought out his next victim.

Lassiter was running out of shells, and not hearing any firing from the end of the shack he didn't want to face Murdoch and the dynamite-throwing bastard, Skeeter, on his own if the pair of them decided to make a break for it. It would be healthier for him, he thought, if he joined up with Clanton and the rest of the Slash Y crew. He began to sidle away from his position, ready to leap to his feet and make a run for it if he saw the red spitting arc of a lighted dynamite stick flying out of the window he had scrambled through.

Bob, lying on his side, reloading his rifle, suddenly felt something sharp and cold dig into his back. He gasped with pain and dropped his rifle. The pain flooded all over his body as Brown Bear thrust the knife in deeper. He held Bob face down in the dirt till his legs stopped their twitching and he finally choked on his own blood. Brown Bear got to his feet, now there was only Clanton and Lassiter to deal with here. Then he would ride to Montana and find this Mr Surtees, Clanton's boss, who thought a 'breed wasn't worth the cut a white man was being paid. He would show him Clanton's scalp, to give him an idea how he was going to die. Brown Bear could hear Clanton firing just beyond a broken-wheeled wagon. He gripped his knife almost lovingly, savouring the sweet moment of revenge of the first cut at Clanton's scalp.

'Do you reckon I've upset Brown Bear enough for him to have gone and had hard words with Clanton, Skeeter?' Murdoch said. 'Him and his two boys ain't been firin' at us for a few minutes now.'

'Could be, Murdoch,' replied Skeeter. 'Come to think of it, Lassiter, for some reason's quit firin'. And there ain't as many guns cuttin' loose at us from the front. I opine we'll never get a better chance of gettin' out of this hole we've found our-selves in.'

'The only way to find that out,' said Murdoch, 'is to step outside an' put it to the test. Give me your pistol, Skeeter, that'll leave you both hands free to throw your fire-crackers.'

Skeeter handed over his pistol then lit the inch or two of cheroot he had left in his mouth. He drew on it till the end glowed red, applied it to the two fuses and threw them through the hole in the wall.

Before the dust of the twin explosions had settled, Murdoch was out into the open. He stood straddle-legged, pistols weaving from light to left, looking for likely targets. Skeeter joined him, holding two more sticks of dynamite.

'So far so good, Murdoch,' he said. 'What's the plan now?'

'There ain't any plan,' Murdoch growled, still looking every which way. 'Except gettin' back to Montana, *pronto,* and settin' Rancher Surtees on the road to the hangin' tree. Ritchie can't complain if Clanton ain't swingin' alongside his boss, we ain't miracle workers. We'll have put an end to the rustlin' of his cows, that oughta make him happy.'

'I've a coupla horses in the brush at the other side of the creek,' Skeeter said. 'So we don't have to go to the horse lines. I reckon Clanton, the 'breed, Lassiter and what's left of their gang are grabbin' mounts and gettin' to hell out of it, fast, before some Canadian lawmen come ridin' in.'

'Let's go then,' Murdoch said. 'We shoot everything that moves against us.' He grinned, fiercely at Skeeter. 'And you, *amigo,* blow up everything that's standin'', OK?'

A nerve in Clanton's temple began to tic. Where the hell was Stu, he thought, angrily. He'd had time to belly crawl all the way round the fort. Was he having difficulty in persuading the 'breed to fall in with his plan? And Bob bad ceased firing. He could be only reloading. He couldn't see him hunkered down beyond the busted wagon. But why was he feeling so edgy?

The two explosions gave him a start. It sounded as though the bastards in the shack were staging a breakout. The tic became a pulsating ache. Where were the sounds of the guns cutting loose at the regulators from that end of the shack? He stood up; he would have to find out for himself just what was making him so jumpy. He turned and saw Brown Bear standing only feet away from him. It didn't need the knife the 'breed was brandishing to tell him what his intentions were. The wild-eyed face gave him the blood-chilling message. He'd had every right to be feeling nervous.

A cursing Brown Bear leapt at Clanton. Clanton brought up his rifle in a frantic attempt to ward off what Brown Bear had hoped to be a killing thrust now he had lost the edge of surprise. With a flashing of sparks the knife slid off the rifle barrel and slashed open Clanton's left arm from elbow to wrist, causing him to drop the rifle, with some cursing of his own.

Heedless of the pain, Clanton grabbed hold of Brown Bear's knife hand in a desperate struggle to keep the blade from doing its deadly work. Brown Bear's burning hate gave him the extra strength needed to force Clanton's hand back, bringing the knife closer to his throat.

Lassiter, coming round the corner of the shack, saw the struggling figures, noticing that Clanton was about to lose out. It was of no interest to him why the 'breed had the urge to kill Clanton, but he had no hesitation in knowing who he should side with. Clanton, even wounded, was another gun which would help to keep Murdoch and Skeeter from getting too close to him on the trail back to Montana. The 'breed hadn't that problem of getting out of Canada, he could lose himself among the trees. As unfeeling as though he was shooting cans off a rail fence, Lassiter put two shells into Brown Bear's head. Brown Bear grunted with pain, and died, falling away from a panting, drawn-faced Clanton.

Clanton was hurriedly tying his bandanna round his lower arm in an attempt to stop the fast-flowing blood as Lassiter came up to him. He knew the stone-faced son-of-a-bitch hadn't saved his life out of any goodness in his heart. Lassiter needed him as much as he needed Lassiter. He would be no more hankering to face Murdoch and Skeeter on his own than he was.

'Thanks for downin' the 'breed,' he said. 'The bastard had my throat all but opened.' He tried to look grateful as though Lassiter had been full of good intentions coming to his aid. 'I reckon it's time we got to hell outa here, Monte,' he said. 'Before those two dogs work their way round here with their dynamite sticks. I ain't in no fit state to take them on in a stand-up fight.' And with all the blood he was losing he was in no fit state to make the hard, fast ride back to Red Butte. If he lagged behind on the trail, Lassiter would kiss him goodbye to save his own dirty neck. Unless, Clanton thought, he could offer Lassiter something that would make him want to stick by him.

'I know I owe you money, Monte,' he said, 'but as you can see we ain't goin' to make any here any more. What we had goin' up here is finished. Though if you ride with me to Red Butte we can get our hands on enough cash to set us up real fine for the rest of our natural.'

Lassiter gave him a quizzical look. 'What do we do, rob the town bank?'

Clanton shook his head. 'Naw,' he said. 'We take it off my boss, Mitch Surtees. He's got a safe in the ranch house stacked high with cash. When those regulators ride into Red Butte, Surtees's days are numbered. Of course, Surtees won't be on his own at the ranch, but it's shame to let all that money go unspent.'

Lassiter smiled. 'A real cryin' shame, Clanton,' he said. 'Let's go and make tracks to get it. I'll give you a hand to get on to your horse.'

Murdoch and Skeeter looked down at Brown Bear's body against a backdrop of burning, collapsing buildings, overhung by a pall of black smoke drifting high and wide on the light breeze.

'Skeeter,' Murdoch said. 'I read somewhere about a man's pride could bring him down. M'be they're not the exact words but the 'breed lyin' there sure proves it.'

'Pity Clanton didn't have a bit more pride,' Skeeter said. He pointed to the dark stain on the ground. 'Though that ain't the 'breed's blood. It looks as if Brown Bear stuck his knife into Clanton, before, I reckon Lassiter blew a hole in his head. M'be Clanton will run outa blood by the time he reaches Red Butte, save us a job.'

'It's time we were headin' in that direction, Skeeter,' Murdoch said. 'We've raised all the hell we can here. We'll contact Mr Ritchie and put a smile on his face by tellin' him he can arrange a hangin' party; his neighbour, Mr Surtees, and his straw boss bein' the main guests, and Lassiter, if he ain't halfway to Texas by now. I opine it was him and Clanton we saw ridin' out.'

Three hours after Murdoch and Skeeter

had left what remained of Fort Whoop-up, Pete, Doug Pevril and the two boys rode into the camp. They drew up their mounts and took in the still smouldering, smoking, scene of devastation.

'Those boys don't do things by half, do they, Pete?' the rancher said.

'They sure don't, that's a fact,' replied Pete. 'I can report to my inspector there is no longer a place called Fort Whoop-up.'

Doug Pevril turned to his grandsons. 'Boys,' he said, 'you both scout around till you find the horses, they must be bedded down nearby; there ain't enough rustlers still alive to drive them to Montana. Me and the constable have work to do here.' He swung out of his saddle, and said, 'Since I met up with Mr Murdoch and Mr Skeeter, I seemed to have spent most of my time plantin' dead men. The pair of them ain't let me down; they've left two more bodies to bury over there. And I reckon if I look around there could be some more of their handiwork lying around.'

Fourteen

Surtees, working on his tally books, looked up sharply as the den door crashed open. The what-the-hell glare froze when death's-head-faced Clanton, followed by his new hireling, Lassiter, stormed into the room.

He knew he was about to hear some bad news from Clanton, but not the disastrous, end-of-his-world news he listened to, ashen-faced, with unbelieving shock. 'So me and Lassiter intend ridin' south,' he heard Clanton say, as if from afar. 'And we're takin' that cash you got stashed in the safe with us. To kinda compensate us for all the hassle we've just been put through across the line.' Picturing the fearful scene of grim-faced, hanging men closing in on him, it took Surtees's numbed brain several seconds to register what Clanton had said.

He flared up in mad anger. 'Take my money?' he yelled. 'I'll see you both in Hell first, you sonsuvbitches!' He grabbed wildly to get at the pistol in the top drawer of his desk.

Lassiter was faster, his pistol barked once and Surtees was knocked hard against the back of his chair by a bullet in the centre of his forehead. He slipped sideways to lie draped over one of the chair's arms, beyond the humiliation of a public hanging.

'Get the fat bastard's safe open, Clanton,' Lassiter snarled. *'Pronto!* We didn't see any hands ridin' in but some could be close enough to the house to have heard the shot.'

Clanton picked up the bunch of keys lying on top of the desk and, kneeling down at the safe, unlocked the heavily reinforced metal door. Lassiter's eyes widened at the sight of the neat piles of dollars Clanton was stuffing into his saddle-bags. Enough cash, he thought, to buy half the longhorns in Texas.

'That's the lot, Monte,' Clanton said,

fastening the straps on the bags. He stood up. 'We'll split it up once we're well clear of Red Butte.'

Lassiter favoured him with a hard-faced grin. 'I've a better idea, Clanton. We divi up right here, I get a hundred per cent, and you get a bullet.'

Clanton dirty-mouthed and grabbed for his gun in a forlorn chance to beat a man with his pistol already in his hand. He took Lassiter's shot full in the chest, spinning him round, then falling over the body of his former boss, on his way to join up with him in Hell.

'No hard feelin's, Clanton,' Lassiter said. 'It just made better business sense to me. After all, you gave Purvis the same deal.' He bent down and slung the well-filled saddle-bags over his shoulder and, with pistol still drawn, he made it to his horse, unchallenged by any Slash Y crew.

Murdoch groaned and eased his great bulk in the saddle. 'Skeeter,' he said, 'I did tell you we were gettin' too old for this game, didn't I? And that makes me not to want to hard-ass it all over the territory to find Ritchie's spread. We'll swing round to hit the Red Butte trail and ask Big Meg to point out the way to the Double Circle. If that's OK by you, *amigo?*'

'It's OK by me,' replied Skeeter. 'You're the planmakin' *hombre* of the team. Do you think we oughta tell Big Meg about Lassiter?' he asked.

'Naw,' replied Murdoch. 'It'll only upset her knowing the rat is in the territory. Though by now I reckon him and Clanton are well on their way to the Wyomin' border. We'll let Ritchie know about them; he could have arrest warrants posted on them, bein' it seems he's a man who likes all the loose ends tied up.'

Lassiter felt real lucky, lucky enough to make a change in his plans. Instead of heading for Texas and setting himself up as a big rancher with his unexpected windfall, he would ride into Red Butte and wait for

Murdoch and Skeeter to show up. They couldn't be that far behind him and would, he judged, be calling in on the town marshal. No one in town knew he worked for the Slash Y so if news of the killings at the ranch broke in town he couldn't be linked with them. And Red Butte was the last place the regulators would expect him to be. Lassiter smiled for real. He had everything going for him. Those two bastards were due for one big surprise, just before he gunned them down from some alley. Then it would be a slow, easy ride south.

Meg drew back into the dry goods store in alarm on seeing Lassiter walking along the opposite boardwalk holding a rifle. She saw him stop on the porch of the barber's shop and sit down well back in the shade. Her face grimmed over, he was all set to do some shooting. Somehow the son-of-a-bitch must have found out Murdoch and Skeeter were in the territory.

She had done all she could to warn

Murdoch and Skeeter when they rode back into Red Butte that Lassiter was here. Told Luke to keep a watchful eye out for them. Even described their likeness to the blacksmith if they stabled their horses in his barn and to pass on the message that their friend, Mr Lassiter, was in town. Leastways, as far as she could see, he had no Slash Y men backing him up. Meg's skirt scuffed the dust as she hurried back to the rooming-house.

'Are we goin' to call on the local law, Murdoch,' Skeeter asked, as they swung in on to Main Street.

'Naw,' replied Murdoch. 'Let Ritchie do the paperwork. And besides, the marshal could look unfriendly on us considerin' we've done what should have been his job, cleanin' his territory of rustlers. Big Meg's place it is.'

Lassiter saw them approaching and quickly stepped down from the porch into the alley to wait for Murdoch and Skeeter to ride past him. He was ideally placed to back-shoot them both. Lassiter felt like doing a jig at all the luck he was having.

Meg left the rooming-house by the back entrance, carrying a double-barrelled shotgun, still moving in the same urgent speed. Cutting through back lots she came on to Main Street below the barber's shop. She was all set to sneak up on Lassiter and march him at gun point to the marshal's office and denounce him as a wanted outlaw. Lassiter would probably tell the marshal how she had earned her living before coming to Red Butte; she would live with that as long as it meant Murdoch and Skeeter staying alive. Meg stopped dead in her tracks, Lassiter wasn't on the porch.

Frantic-eyed she looked up and down Main Street for a sighting of him, and saw Murdoch and Skeeter slow-riding their horses ahead of her. Then Lassiter came into her view, stepping out of an alley opposite her, rifle to his shoulder.

'Murdoch!' she screamed. 'Behind you!' And jerked the triggers of the gun from waist-high. The wild discharges missed Lassiter and shattered the windows of the barber shop instead.

Meg's shriek, the shotgun blast, the sound of breaking glass set Lassiter's nerves jumping, unsteadying his aim and the shell that should have torn its killing way through Murdoch's broad back, hit him in the shoulder. Murdoch gasped and sagged in his saddle, clutching at his wounded arm. Skeeter spun round, pistol in his hand, thumbing back the hammer.

A cursing Lassiter wasted a few, fatal seconds in deciding whether to fire at the crazy bitch with the shotgun, or take on Skeeter. Skeeter's rapid shots ended his dilemma, and his run of good luck for all time. Skeeter kept firing until the hammer clicked on an empty shell and Lassiter lay stretched out in the dirt as dead as any man can be.

Meg ran across to Murdoch. 'Are you're OK?' she said in a voice full of concern.

'Just winged, Meg,' Murdoch groaned.

'Though if it hadn't been for you I would've been more than winged, that's for sure.'

'Think nothing of it, Murdoch,' Meg said. 'You stopped that bastard from killing one of my girls, I've only paid you back what I owe you. Now let's get you to my place so I can see to that arm.'

'I'll pay a call on the marshal,' Skeeter said. 'Explain to him what the shootin' was about, and what we've been doin' across in Canada. Then I'll ask him to point me in the direction of the Double Circle so I can tell Ritchie he's a hangin' to look forward to once he's sent his boys to pick up Surtees.'

Murdoch was sitting in a big easy chair in Meg's parlour, arm bandaged up, chatting to Meg when Skeeter, all smiles came into the room.

'The assignment is all cleared up, pard,' he said. 'Surtees and Clanton are dead. While I was in the marshal's office the Slash Y's Chinee cook came in, all worked up, and told us best as he could in his heathen tongue and part American, that he'd found his boss's and Clanton's body lyin' in den in the big house with bullet holes in them. And a safe emptied of all its cash.'

'It looks as though Lassiter did us a good turn,' Murdoch said. 'That won't lie easy with him when he's stokin' up the fires of Hell, Skeeter.'

'The marshal found the cash in Lassiter's saddle-bags,' Skeeter said. 'Then, bein' that he could see I was worryin' about my partner bein' shot, he rode out to the Double Circle to tell Ritchie the good news. Though I reckon he only wants to grab a bit of the glory tellin' Ritchie that all the rustlers have been accounted for.'

Murdoch beamed. 'Were you frettin' about me, pard?'

'Yeah I was worried, a mite,' replied Skeeter. 'It could have been me who took Lassiter's slug and I ain't carryin' the beef to be winged safely in no place.' He looked at Meg. 'Is he fit enough to ride, Meg,' he said. 'Because I'm as sure as hell not about to break in another partner, I'd rather herd sheep.'

Meg smiled. She didn't feel like smiling. She would have liked to have told them that keeping sheep wasn't a bad idea. Bettered their chances of dying with their boots off. But she was in no position to lecture anyone on how they should live their lives. She had chosen to be a whore.

'Let the big ox rest up a few days, Skeeter, for the wound to knit together. Then you can ride out and raise hell in someone else's backyard,' she said, still false smiling.

The publishers hope that this book has given you enjoyable reading. Large Print Books are especially designed to be as easy to see and hold as possible. If you wish a complete list of our books please ask at your local library or write directly to:

Dales Large Print Books
Magna House, Long Preston,
Skipton, North Yorkshire.
BD23 4ND

This Large Print Book for the partially sighted, who cannot read normal print, is published under the auspices of
THE ULVERSCROFT FOUNDATION

THE ULVERSCROFT FOUNDATION

... we hope that you have enjoyed this Large Print Book. Please think for a moment about those people who have worse eyesight problems than you ... and are unable to even read or enjoy Large Print, without great difficulty.

You can help them by sending a donation, large or small to:

**The Ulverscroft Foundation,
1, The Green, Bradgate Road,
Anstey, Leicestershire, LE7 7FU,
England.**
or request a copy of our brochure for more details.

The Foundation will use all your help to assist those people who are handicapped by various sight problems and need special attention.

Thank you very much for your help.